PLANTS AND CRIME

PLANTS AND CRIME

A Green Mystique Forensic Mystery Companion

ALAN GRAHAM

GREEN MYSTIQUE PRESS

GREEN MYSTIQUE PRESS
greenmystiquepress.com

PLANTS AND CRIME:
A GREEN MYSTIQUE FORENSIC MYSTERY COMPANION

ISBN 978-1-7363184-1-6

Book design by cj Madigan

In memory of Walter H. Lewis (1930-2020),

former Director of the Missouri Botanical Garden Herbarium,

professor at Washington University, St. Louis,

respected colleague,

and valued contributor

to the Ruidoso plane crash project

described in this volume

CONTENTS

FROM NONFICTION TO FICTION

A NOTE TO THE READER

Throughout my career as a botanist I have been fascinated not just by plants themselves but also by their usefulness in answering scientific and forensic questions. My Green Mystique mystery novels—*Gateway to Murder*, *Season of Discontent*, and *Mass Extinctions*—use a fictional investigator, John Ramming of the St. Louis Division of Criminal Investigation Services, to explore the ways plant evidence might be applied to the investigation of three fictional criminal cases. This companion book explains the science behind the novels and describes four real life puzzles that plant material has helped to solve. Together, I hope the four books illuminate the immense richness and intricacy of plant life, as well as the diverse and sometimes surprising role plants play in clarifying mysteries of all kinds.

Alan Graham
December 2020

JOHN RAMMING AT WORK: RUIDOSO AND *DAS RHEINGOLD*

RUIDOSO AND
DAS RHEINGOLD

With recognition comes responsibilities. The words hung in John Ramming's mind as he sat down in his office, turned on his computer, and began to prepare his paper for the American Society of Criminology conference being held in St. Louis in three months' time. A week in length, the ASC conference was one of the world's most distinguished annual gatherings of criminologists, attracting experts in a wide variety of specialties from around the globe. Morning sessions were devoted to lectures and discussions, afternoons to readings and demonstrations; several evenings were scheduled for dinners and award presentations, others left free for attendees to meet and mingle on their own.

The conference was planned for May, at which point participants visiting the city might be lucky enough to avoid the worst of both its sometimes chilly winters and its humid summers. Now, on a Sunday afternoon in late February, it was cold outside and, with the building in off-hours energy-saving mode, inside as well. The light from the office window, pale and thin, made the space look oddly desolate. Ramming's office was as likely to be bustling on Sunday as on a weekday. When the Division was deep in a case distinctions like days of the week didn't apply. But today, all was silence. The caseload of St. Louis's Division of Criminal Investigation Services (DCIS), where Ramming served as Commanding Officer, was in a rare lull. Ramming had no doubt that would change, and change soon. In the meantime, the unusually quiet spell gave him a chance to prepare for his ASC presentation, something he'd necessarily put off in the hectic months just past.

Even in lulls, conference papers weren't the kind of task he approached with enthusiasm. In fact, he had initially ignored both the ASC's public call for proposals and the personal invitation from the organization's chair. Then Andrew Hardin, head of the DCIS, had made his wishes felt. Always conscious of political optics and funding streams, Hardin had urged him to "show your face in the outside world. You know how useful it is for me to be able to remind the powers-that-be how distinguished you are. With budgets being cut left and right, the more people we can impress the better. And besides, I don't need to tell you that with recognition comes responsibilities."

Ramming had silently bristled, but he couldn't entirely disagree. DCIS had a degree of autonomy that his counterparts in other units and agencies envied, and no group or function was immune from funding cuts or even dissolution. The high success rate DCIS achieved on its complex cases spoke for itself, but visibility was useful too.

Some of the colleagues who attended ASC each year looked forward to it and to conferences, colloquia and conventions generally. They welcomed the chance to make useful connections, exchange new ideas, eat and drink at their employer's expense, and, in some cases, misbehave in ways that were difficult to get away with at home. Ramming wasn't one of them. A singularly private person, he found superficial exchanges exhausting. He knew, without being able to change it, that his natural intensity and perfectionism could feel forbidding and that others approached him with respect and even caution. Then there were the challenges of his sardonic sense of humor and his thick (for some listeners, nearly incomprehensible) Scottish brogue. DCIS had gradually evolved into a like-minded assemblage of individuals who, for their own reasons and in their own ways, were just as driven as Ramming himself and who tolerated, even appreciated, each other's quirks. Away from these familiar colleagues and the almost maniacal intensity they shared while on a case, Ramming rarely felt fully at ease.

That was one reason he hated being pulled away from his work, but not the most important one. Crime didn't pause for criminologists' convenience. Ever since the time, four years before, that his absence for a conference had coincided with one of the most challenging cases ever assigned to the DCIS, he'd felt an obsessive need to justify anything and everything that took him away. No one but Ramming himself demanded that justification. It was just a deep inner need, a drive to prove that the sacrifices of time and focus were worth their possible cost.

At least this year's ASC was being held in St. Louis. He didn't have to stay in a hotel beside hundreds of other attendees and the America's Center conference site was only six blocks away from the office. It would be possible to make himself available on short notice if an unusually demanding case required his personal attention during the course of the conference. Even if that didn't happen, it was comforting to know that he'd be able to return home each night. Sitting alone amid the thunderous chords of Wagner—he was currently listening yet again to *Das Rheingold*, his favorite—helped him keep his patience, always in short supply, and maintain his mental balance, which was always being pushed to the edge.

Two hours later, he finished the draft introduction to his conference paper, sat back in his office chair and stretched. The subject he'd chosen—the use of plants and plant material in criminal investigation—was important yet, to Ramming's mind, oddly overlooked. ASC was an elite gathering, but even the colleagues most expert in other aspects of forensics tended to be unaware of the arsenal of approaches forensic botany offered for historical research, criminal investigation, and more. Instances in which forensic botany had been used were relatively rare, yet each demonstrated its power in determining guilt or innocence, separating truth from supposition, replacing hypotheses with conclusions.

Ramming pulled the introduction text from its tray on the printer and returned to the desk. To his surprise, he was eager to keep going. Outlining the basics of plant structure and the ways plant material could be used in a way that would be clear to listeners likely to be unfamiliar with both was a satisfyingly intricate challenge. And unfamiliar as they were, the case studies he had chosen were fascinating to revisit. Mass extinctions; the Neanderthals' humanity or lack thereof; the Lindbergh baby kidnapping; and the 1989 Ruidoso, New Mexico plane crash: plants held a key to understanding all four of these mysteries and more.

Absorbed in the work, Ramming didn't see the light fade from yellow-gray to the pending darkness of night. By the time he looked away from the glow of the computer screen, it was twilight. Time to head home, have some dinner, and prepare for the week. As he closed up the office and made his way home, his mind continued to sift through the material for his presentation and its subsequent publication.

Unusually for a highly observant man, Ramming barely noticed that it was Ruidoso rather than *Das Rheingold* that he was looking forward to exploring further that evening.

THE REAL DEAL:
THE USES OF PLANT EVIDENCE

Presented by John Ramming

American Society of Criminology Conference

St. Louis, Missouri

LAYING THE GROUNDWORK

Investigations where accuracy, reputations, or lives are on the line require a wide range of evidence to establish a reliable basis for reaching conclusions and rendering oftentimes momentous decisions. There is no room for error. Too much is riding on the verdict. One widely used source of this evidence is the plant material associated with a crime or other event. Crucial information may come from familiar plants like ferns, gymnosperms (cone-bearing plants), and angiosperms (flowering plants). Useful evidence may also come from less obvious botanical sources: bacteria, algae, and fungi, and plant remains such as spores, pollen, seeds, trichomes (hairs), phytoliths (crystals), and vegetative parts such as wood, other kinds of plant tissue, and cells. Such material can help us understand historical events, such as mass extinctions including that of the dinosaurs some 65 million years ago, and also answer questions such as how "human" were our early relations, the Neanderthals, compared to us in behavior as well as physical structure.

Plant data can also solve mysteries closer to us in both distance and time. The subfield of forensic botany deals specifically with the application of plant data to the solution of crimes or resolution of charges adjudicated in a court of law. Plant fragments may help identify the time, place, and conditions of the crime; determine if objects at the scene are in place or have been moved; and verify or contradict explanations and alibis. Among real-life examples are claims of a design flaw in the engine of a plane that crashed killing two people near Ruidoso, New Mexico in 1989, and the kidnapping and death of the infant Charles Lindbergh, Jr. in Hopewell, New Jersey in 1932.

Almost ubiquitous in occurrence, plants have been used worldwide in investigations of these kinds for centuries. This paper discusses the types of plant materials that may factor into such cases as well as their application in the four inquiries referenced above.

METHODS AND MATERIALS

As demonstrated from the cases of early fictional detectives such as Auguste Dupin and Sherlock Holmes to hundreds of modern fictional and documentary investigation dramas, physical evidence is a key tool in the understanding of criminal cases. It is also foundational in non-criminal inquiries such as scientific research and civil litigation. Physical (sometimes called material) evidence may be clearly visible, as with the pieces of a plane recovered after an air disaster, the weapon found at a crime scene,

or the barrels of chemical waste discovered to have been
illegally buried in the water contamination case at the
center of Jonathan Haar's *A Civil Action*. It may also appear
in the form of trace evidence, the microscopic and other
small particles barely visible to the naked eye. Hair and
other fibers, flakes or fragments of substances such as
paint that may be transferred during an event, and grains
of gunpowder and other residues are all common forms
of trace evidence, as are many minute plant components.

Pollen and spores: the basics

Pollen is the sperm-bearing element in the reproduction of
seed plants (the angiosperms and gymnosperms mentioned
above). Spores are small reproductive structures of the
non-seed plants such as ferns, bryophytes, algae, and fungi.

Pollen is most familiar as the cause of allergies to plants like
juniper, grasses, and ragweed and to mold spores produced
by the fungi. With these allergies there often come secondary
sensitivities to substances such as dust and heightened
touch-reaction to plant acids (poison ivy), oils, and other
chemicals. Of course, pollen is also the material gathered by
bees to make honey. Study of this group of approximately
20,000 insects constitutes the field of melittology.

However, pollen and spores are important in fields besides
allergenic medicine and melittology. These fields include
botanical taxonomy (the classification and identification of
plants); systematics (the study of evolutionary pathways
and relationships); climatology (climate change and global

warming); and archaeology and anthropology (reconstructing site environments, land practices, plant use; determining the source, time, and place of origin of cultivated plants; and tracking the migration of humans). The study of pollen and spores, called palynology from the Greek word for fine dust or flour, is further used to understand the dietary habits of ancient organisms through analysis of stomach contents. These particles also have a wide range of geological applications. For example, pollen and spores can help determine depositional environments, age, and correlation of strata in oil exploration.[1] Last but not least, both pollen and spores are important in investigative and judicial proceedings, our principal interest here.

If pollination is by wind, and depends on random chance for the pollen to land on the female cone or on the female part of the flower, it is often produced in prodigious quantities, as in the gymnosperms *Juniperus* (juniper or cedar) and *Pinus* (pine), and in the angiosperm family Poaceae (grasses, Figure 1) and *Ambrosia*, or ragweed. This pollen is typically small, light, dry, and smooth, characteristics that facilitate unimpeded airborne transport.

Pollination effected by insects (bees, moths, beetles) and other animals (bats, hummingbirds) is more efficient; thus, such pollen is usually produced in smaller quantities (Figure 2, *Hibiscus*). In these cases the grains are often larger, containing greater protoplasm and reward for the pollinating vector; ornate, with spines or other projecting structures; sticky;

and occasionally featuring long hair-like strands, called viscin threads, for attaching to the animal or insect pollinator.

Fungal spores and other fungal remains (Graham, 1962) in addition to pollen grains are now expanding the investigative arsenal through a field called forensic mycology (Hawksworth and Wiltshire, 2011). There are three principle groups of fungi:

- The Basidiomycetes, which comprise the common mushrooms and shelf fungi, have spores that are typically small (about 5-10 micrometers), thick-walled, and dark in color. This group is primarily found growing on land.

- Also primarily terrestrial, the Ascomycetes (*Penicillium* is one of the better known) are larger and multicellular. Individual types in this group can further be recognized by whether the spores are unicellular or multicellular, and borne individually or in chains.

- The third group, Phycomycetes (water molds), is mostly aquatic and its spores thin-walled and delicate.

In all three groups, the hyphae—one of two main fungus building-blocks—also preserve and can often be distinguished (e.g., thick-walled, septate, and uninucleate in most stages of the Ascomycetes; thick-walled, septate, and binucleate in most Basidiomycetes; and non-septate, thin, and multinucleate in the Phycomycetes). Thus, with spores, hyphae are also part of the investigative arsenal.

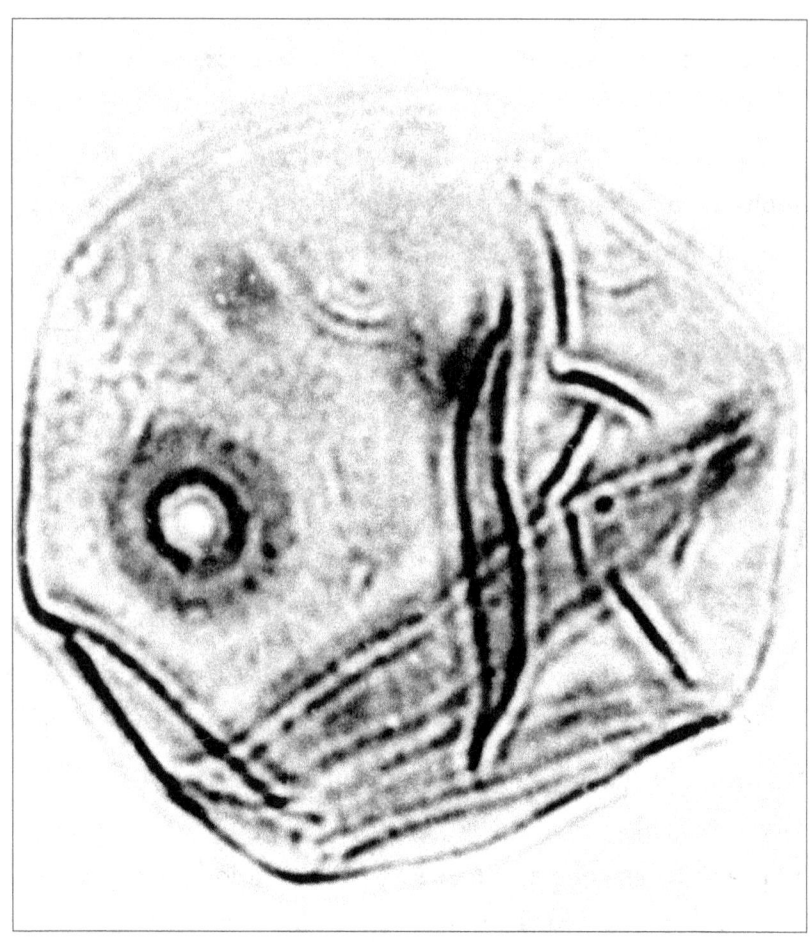

Figure 1. Fossil pollen of Poaceae (grass family) from
the Pliocene Gatun Formation of Panama (ca. 28µ). The
circular pore is for emission of the pollen tube carrying
the sperm nuclei and is surrounded by a thickened
annulus. The lines are compression folds and creases.

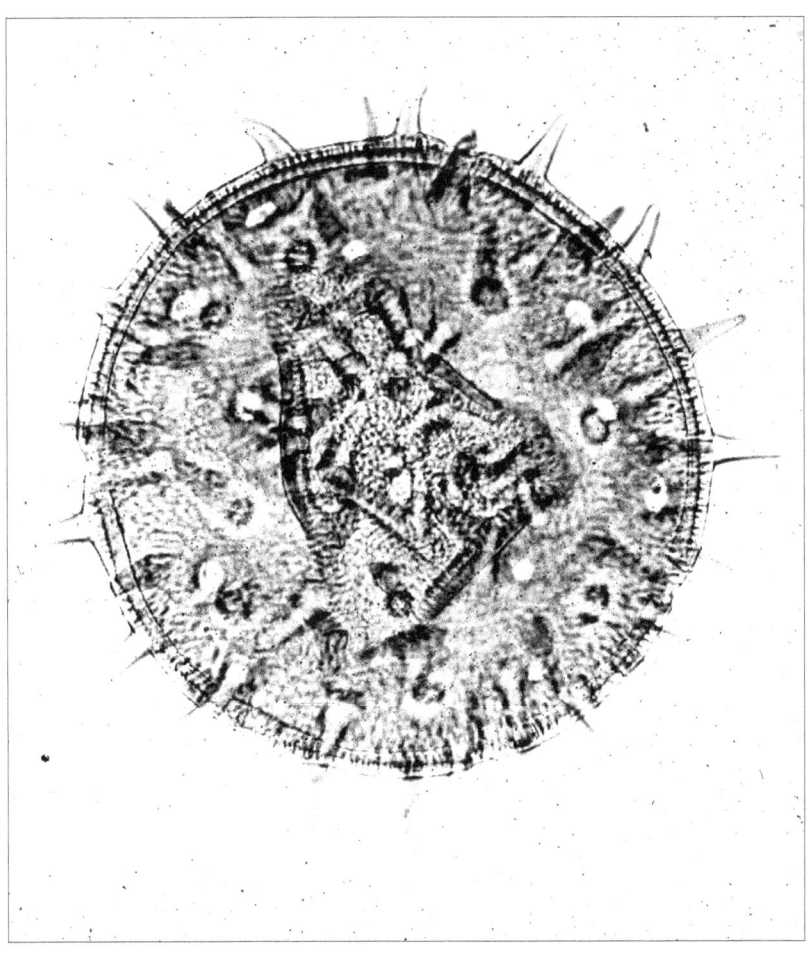

Figure 2. Modern pollen of *Hibiscus militaris* from the Missouri Botanical Garden (MBG) herbarium used to establish a pollen and spore reference collection for taxonomic study and identification of fossil specimens (cf. Figure 3; ca. 100 μ).

Along with bacteria, the fungi initiate the disintegration
of organic material including the human remains around
which some criminal investigations center. Each organism
proceeds at different rates and appears at different times
in the process of decay. Thus, their use in investigative
plant science and forensics is similar to that for pollen.
Taxonomically, they can help establish relationships and
evolutionary history; forensically, they can help pinpoint the
time since death and the season, place, and habitat of a crime.

Applications of palynology

Some of the applications of palynology follow.

1. *Most plants produce either pollen grains or
spores.* Hence, palynology can be applied to events
occurring virtually anywhere and involving virtually
all major forms of the Earth's vegetation.

2. *Pollen grains and spores are released to the atmosphere
during wind pollination, fall as the pollen and spore rain,
and are widely distributed by atmospheric currents.* In turn,
the pathways of such currents are often identified and the
direction and rate-of-flow determined by the pollen and spore
content as measured by samplers at airports, on the roofs
of hospitals, and at meteorological stations. It is this data
that helps estimate the direction, source, and time of arrival
of ash from volcanic eruptions and identify radiation from
atomic power plant disasters and clandestine nuclear testing.

3. *Each spore and grain of pollen is surrounded by
a resistant cell wall.* This cell wall is called an exine in

pollen (angiosperms and gymnosperms) or spore wall in the non-seed plants (algae, fungi, bryophytes, and ferns and related groups). These walls are almost indestructible when deposited in rapidly accumulating sediments, which reduces oxidation, and under acid conditions, which reduces microbial degradation. Hence, pollen and spores preserve relatively well, facilitating their use in a wide range of inquiries about events past and present.

4. Pollen and spores readily fossilize. A sample of geological sediment about the size of a marble can yield 100,000 or more plant microfossils representing 100 or more types.

The sediments in which fossilized pollen and spores are found include volcanic ash, clay, mud, silt, and ice. Where the sediments are highly organic they may be converted to lignite (pre-coal deposits) and eventually to bituminous (soft) and anthracite (hard) coal. Thus, fossil spores or spore-like bodies and pollen (Figure 3) are present in a variety of sediments throughout most of the geologic column. Spores are found back to near the beginning of life approximately 3.5 billion years ago. Pollen and other remains of the gymnosperms appear toward the end of the Devonian Period about 350 million years ago and extend to the present; angiosperm fossils range from the early Cretaceous Period approximately 135 million years ago to the present. These fossils can be retrieved from rock cuts made during road construction (Figure 4), river and canyon-side exposures, and well cores. Specimens are processed through a series of acids (HCL for limestone, HF for silicates, HNO_3 for lignin

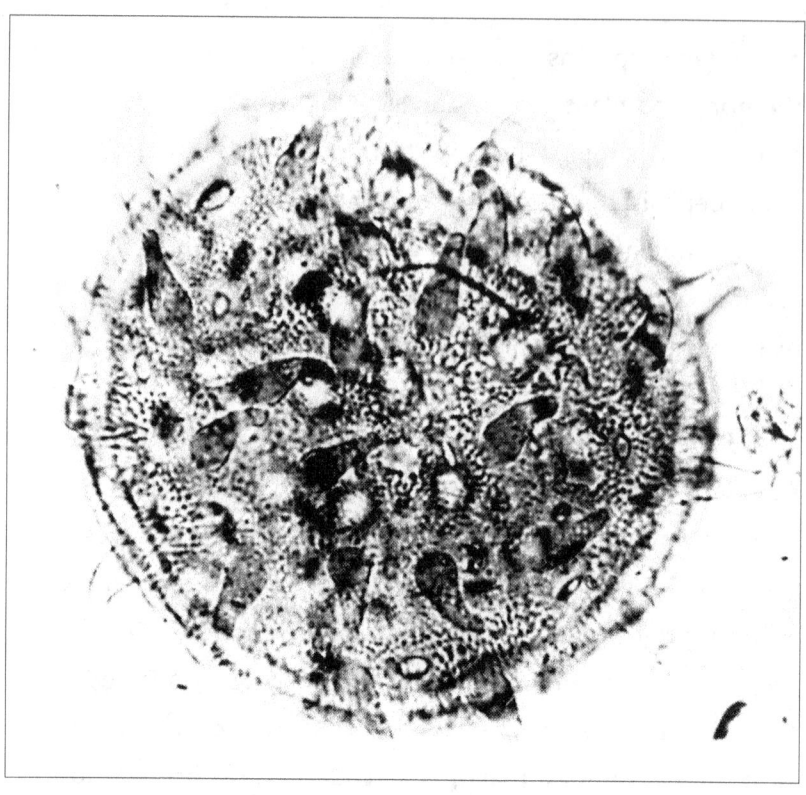

Figure 3. Fossil pollen of *Hibiscus* (Malvaceae) ca. 3.5 Ma years old from the Pliocene Paraje Solo Formation, Veracruz, Mexico. Graham, 1976.

Figure 4. Roadside exposure of the middle Pliocene Paraje Solo Formation near Coatzacoalcos, coastal Veracruz, Mexico with David M. Jarzen (left, Field Museum, Chicago, Cleveland Museum of Natural History) and Enrique Martínez-Hernández (Universidad Nacional Autónoma de México). The dark bands are lenses of lignite deposited in brackish water at the ocean-continent interface. The lighter bands are sandy mineral sediments deposited in slightly deeper marine water when the coastline was further offshore. Cycles of exposure and inundation were due to rise and falls in actual sea level (isostatic changes) and/or rise and fall of the land (relative changes). The oldest sediments are at the bottom road-level part of the section and the youngest at the top (relative ages). The age of middle Pliocene was assigned on the basis of independent evidence from planktic (floating) foraminifer fossils and which globally conforms to ca. 3.5 Ma (absolute radiometric dates were not available). Graham, 1976.

and other organic debris) to dissolve accreted minerals while leaving the acid-resistant pollen and spores intact. Mounted in silicone oil or other inert media, the slides are essentially permanent, lasting for hundreds of years.

Typically, the oldest sediments will be at the bottom of a core or section and the youngest toward the top providing a sequence of *relative* ages: that is, fossils that are "younger than" or "older than" the others. Vertical sampling from a single locality reveals changes at a given site through time, while sampling at multiple localities reveals these changes and the arrangement of the communities of organisms at a single point in time over the landscape. Where organic material is present in the fossils or sediments, radiometric techniques can also provide an *absolute* age in number of years for the lineage, community, ecosystem, and events that tells the general extent, direction, and pace of change. This allows extinctions; humanity-defining behavior in the hominids, Neanderthals, Denisovans, and early Sapiens; and criminal acts to be investigated and dated in relative and real time.

5. Pollen and spores are sufficiently diverse in physical structure and form to allow most families, many genera, and some species to be identified on the basis of their morphology (Figures 5-16). Because these particles are so small, significant magnification is required for such identification. Light microscopy (LM; Figures 5-16) permits examination of their surface features at magnification levels of approximately 1000x, or 1,000 times their actual size, while scanning electron microscopy (SEM; Figure 17) can magnify them to approximately 400,000 times their actual size. Sections of the wall can also be studied by transmission electron microscopy (TEM; Figure 18) at magnification levels of up to 400,000x; with the advent of MicroCT Scanning (μCT) and associated technology, the sections can be combined into three-dimensional images and rotated in space, enhancing the accuracy of identifications and the evolutionary and environmental interpretations scientists base on them. Illustrations of both modern and fossil pollen and spores are presented in the published scientific literature and in online catalogs. Reference material for modern plants is assembled in university or museum herbaria (Graham, 2011; see Figures 4.2 and 4.3 there) where label data provide the identification, geographic distribution, and ecological conditions under which the plants grow. Some herbaria contain 7 million or more of these plants, while some pollen and spore reference collections based on these collections number 25,000 or more species. One of the largest was recently gifted to the Smithsonian Institution, where it is presently housed at the STRI (Smithsonian Tropical Research institute) in Panama (Smithsonian Insider, 2009; Figure 19).

6. *Plants are limited in their geologic age, geographic distribution, and ecological tolerance.* This means individual pollen and spore types and other fossils broadly represent the age, place, set of environmental conditions (climate, altitude, geography, vegetation, soil type, pH, and by implication the associated fauna), and disturbance events at a site being studied. Especially important for forensics

is that the assemblage of pollen and spores can reveal whether the object on or in which they were found has been moved. The location may be indicated not only by the modern pollen and spores that are present, but also by the age of any fossils in adhering sediments, such as mud in pant cuffs or at the heel-sole intersect of shoes. Vegetation maps along with field observations will show what modern plant communities (marsh, grassland, forest, or altered/secondary farmland, parkland, or garden of specific composition) grow, for example, on Carboniferous-age siltstone. Analyses that indicate a substrate of Carboniferous-age siltstone with an existing cover of aquatic and marsh plants will often include sufficient information to pinpoint the original location, season of origin, and transport history of an object under investigation rather precisely.

7. *As part of the search for pollen and spores, other types of plant microfossils may be recovered with proper processing of a sample.* By omitting the HF treatment, for example, silicate crystals called phytoliths may remain, and some are distinctive enough to be identified as to family and genus. The phytoliths of economically important plants like *Zea mays* (corn) from sediments at archaeological sites have contributed valuable information about the time and place of origin of this and other cultivars (Piperno, 2006; Piperno and Pearsall, 1998). They also add to the inventory of plants found on and in various objects, victims, and suspects at crime scenes. The same is true of an aquatic algal group known as diatoms. They have silica in their cell

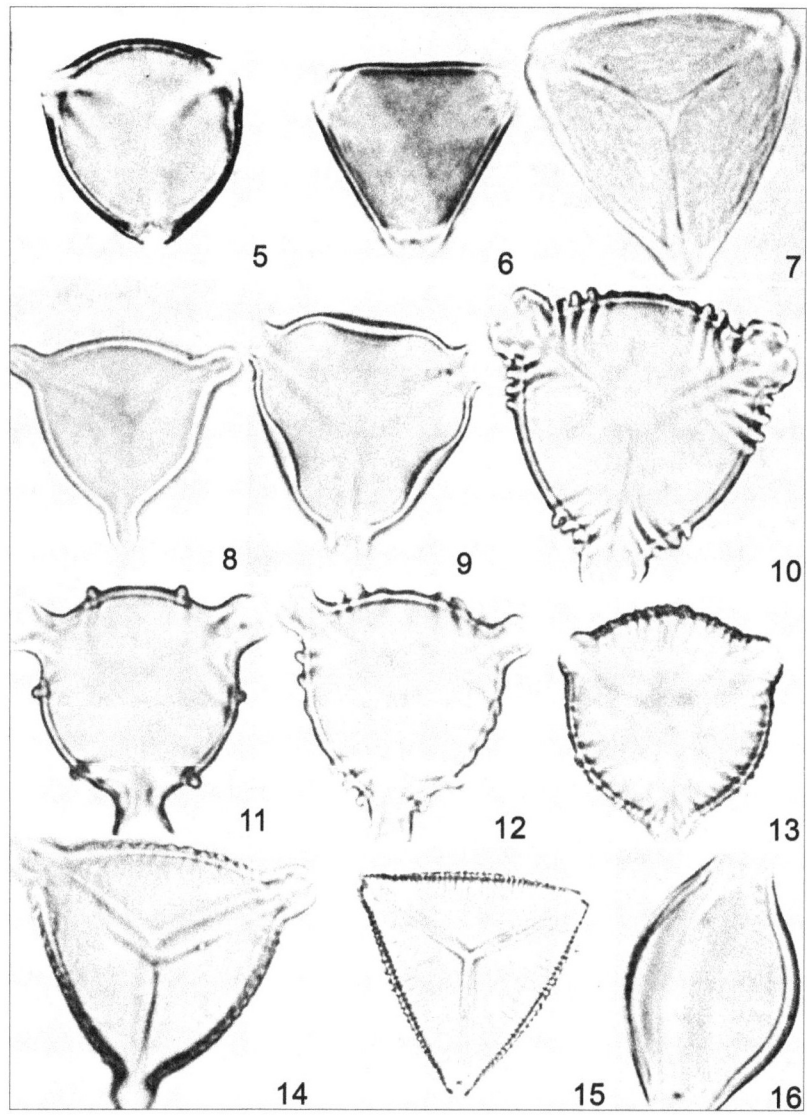

Figure 5-16. Diversity in pollen as shown by species within the single genus *Cuphea* (Lythraceae). 5. *Cuphea epilobiifolia*. 6. *C. spruceana*. 7. *C. melvilla*. 8. *C. aspera*. 9. *C. ramulosa* 10. *C. boissieriana*. 11. *C. campestris*. 12. *C. carthagenensis*. 13. *C. cordata*. 14. *C. lobelioides*. 15. *C. bustamanta*. 16. *C. ingrata*. Reference material was from the MBG and other herbaria. Photographs were taken with light microscopy at ca. 1000x magnification. Average actual size is ca. 25-28μ. Graham et al., 1968.

Figure 17. SEM of *Caesalpinia decapetala* (Fabaceae, = Leguminosae) pollen from reference material at the U.S. National Herbarium (US), Washington. D.C.

Figure 18. Cross-section through the pollen wall (exine) of *Ginoria americana* (Lythraceae) showing the columellae composing the wall. The arrangement of the columellae determines the sculpture pattern seen on the surface (smooth, pitted, striate, reticulate—e.g., Figure 17). Graham et al., 1985.

Figure 19. Pollen and spore reference collection at the STRI (Panama) with curator Carlos Jaramillo. Photograph by Marcos Guerra.

wall and many are distinctive in morphology and ecology. Different marine and freshwater species grow at different depths, temperature, and pH, and can therefore provide useful forensic evidence about the past and present location of objects found in aquatic environments.

Seeds

The evolution of the seed, which occurred in the Devonian Period approximately 350 million years ago, contributed to the gymnosperms replacing non-seed plants as the Earth's dominant land vegetation. The earliest seeds were basic structures consisting of an embryo surrounded by a nutritive layer and a hardened outer protective layer or seed coat. In many gymnosperms today and in the past, the seed coat is mostly unornamented and dispersed primarily by gravity, browsing animals, or wind. In some of those distributed by wind there is a winglike structure, as found in pine, spruce, and fir among others. The gymnosperms reached the zenith of their distribution in the Permian, Triassic, Jurassic, and the earliest part of the Cretaceous Period (circa 290-140 million years ago). This was a time of widespread drought, and many modern gymnosperms retain morphological (structural) and physiological (functional) features reflecting their origin in times of aridity. For example, the needle-like shape and sunken sub-epidermal stomata of leaves reduce water loss from their surfaces. Stomata are openings mostly on the lower leaf surface that allow the entrance of CO_2 for photosynthesis but also let water escape as part of the transpiration stream. This stream is evident as dew and by the comparatively higher humidity in forests compared to sparse and open vegetation.[2]

Similarly, some plants produce resins, non-water soluble substances that harden when exposed to air, which also reduce water loss. Many conifers and some angiosperms, like aspens and willows, are resin-producing. When plant resin fossilizes, the result is called amber, deposits of which dating as far back as the Oligocene and Miocene epochs (some 35 to 15 million years ago) have been found in the Dominican Republic and the Baltic region. Because resin takes time to harden (even more to fossilize), amber often contains inclusions such as pollen, flowers, seeds, trichomes, and even small animals like insects and frogs. As such, it is valued for the information it can contribute to research and investigation as well as for its potential commercial use.

The occasional cross-interest between these applications of resin was reflected in an experience in Chiapas, Mexico:

> The Simojovel resident lowered his gun, smiled broadly if somewhat sheepishly, and said, "Puedes beber de mi pozo." His welcome culminated a long morning of discussion near a bluff bordering the village cemetery. Although unsettling, there had been a faint overlay of conviviality throughout the encounter—the villagers knew we probably meant no harm, and we guessed they probably were not going to execute us, however convenient the site. We had come to the village

of Simojovel to collect rock samples. The bluff
was an exposure of the La Quinta Formation
in an area of Chiapas, Mexico famous for the
plant and animal inclusions of its amber deposits.
Mining rights to the amber had been ceded to
local residents, and although there was no amber
at this site, our presence was an opportunity to
pass an otherwise uneventful morning conversing
and good-naturedly harassing strangers from afar.
It took a while to explain that we really had come
thousands of miles to collect rocks of no apparent value from which we would extract spores
and pollen to reconstruct climates and vegetation that had not existed for millions of years.
Convinced we were probably more harmless
than devious, we were eventually accepted with
the local greeting, "You may drink from my well"
(Graham, 2011, p. ix).

As noted previously, the angiosperms appeared about
134 million years ago and replaced the gymnosperms as
the Earth's prominent group of land plants in part due to
their more highly developed seeds. In the flowering plants
the seed, rather than being borne exposed on the surface
of one of the scales on a cone and passively distributed
by wind or gravity, is enclosed in an ovary that matures
into the fruit. The fruit surface and the seed coat can be
evolutionarily elaborated for dispersal without interfering

with their nutritive and protective functions. This happened extensively in the angiosperms and as a result virtually the entire world was opened for their colonization. Only Antarctica, with its permanent and nearly continuous ice cover, is without vegetation dominated by angiosperms— but even there, the two principal land plants are the angiosperms *Colobanthus quitensis* (the Antarctic pearlwort, Caryophyllaceae) and the grass *Deschampsia antarctica*.

Angiosperm fruits and seeds can be dispersed in a variety of ways.

- In some, specialized cells within the fruit deteriorate as the seeds mature and gases build up. At a certain point the pressure exceeds the strength of the fruit or seed wall and it explodes. Ejected into the air, the seeds are carried beyond the competitive influence and depleted soil nutrients around the older and established parent plants.

- In other instances, the wall of the fruit or seed is coated with a waxy layer impervious to salt water and is dispersed by marine currents. The coconut and other palm fruits remain viable for years in ocean water and may travel thousands of miles between continents and across hemispheres.

- Some fruits and seeds are dispersed by the land animals that consume them. The walls of these fruits and seeds are brightly colored (often red) and fleshy, contain sugars and nutrients, and are impervious to digestive enzymes. They are consumed and gradually dispersed step by step over a long period by slowly migrating land animals, or abruptly over vast distances by migratory birds. Though not a seed-eater itself, the Arctic tern (*Stema paradisaea*) demonstrates how wide-ranging dispersal agents can be. The holder of the world record for migration distance, Arctic terns migrate between the Arctic and Antarctic for an annual round trip of approximately 71,000 kilometers (44,000 miles).

• Angiosperm seeds are also dispersed through human consumption. When recovered from the human stomach seeds can contribute to estimates about "the last supper" such as when (how long ago), where (home, restaurant, and ethnicity of the source), and in what season of the year a meal was eaten. Seeds resistant to the digestive process can be studied in detail with modern methods such as Scanning Electron Microscopy (SEM). For example, in 1997 scientists used SEM to examine a strawberry seed from the stomach contents of a homicide victim that turned out to have a tooth mark still intact. (Bock and Norris, 1997).

• The flowers of many orchids resemble in size, shape, and color pattern the female species of certain insects. Going beyond the pale, the plants further produce chemicals sufficiently similar to the female insect's sex pheromones to attract male insects, who attempt to copulate with the flower. In the confusion seeds are picked up and pollen transferred to the next plant. The same subterfuge occurs in the fungus *Tuber* (the truffle). These fungi exude a chemical similar to the female pig's sex pheromone, and male pigs are used to gather the truffles.

- *Amorphophalus* (Figure 20) and the parasitic *Rafflesia* (Figure 21) produce large, conspicuous flowers that grow low to the ground. Mottled-purple in color, they produce an odor like rotting meat. The smell is strong— and unusual—enough to engender a sensation. When a titan arum (*Amorphophalus titanium*) flower bloomed at the Chicago Botanical Gardens in 2015, visitors lined up to smell it and one floriculturist described its scent as reminding him of road kill, a barnyard, and a dirty diaper, with a hint of mothball. Carrion beetles mistake such flowers for food and crawl over them, helping to disperse the seeds. Like the orchid example this is also primarily a co-evolutionary pollination and seed-dispersal device.[3]

- *Cuphea* (Mexican heather; Figure 22) has seed epidermal cells shaped like tiny microscopic boxes with a trap door over the top. Inside each is a coiled filament (Figure 22, bottom right). When the seeds fall in water they swell, the trap door opens, and the filaments extrude, covering the surface of the seed with a mass of hairs (Figure 22, center right). These hairs act as floats, sticking to passing objects and facilitating dispersal.

Figure 20. *Amorphophallus titanium* (Araceae; with *Pandanus* sp., Pandanaceae, MBG)

Figure 21. *Raffelesia* sp., Malaysia. Photograph from Shirley A. Graham.

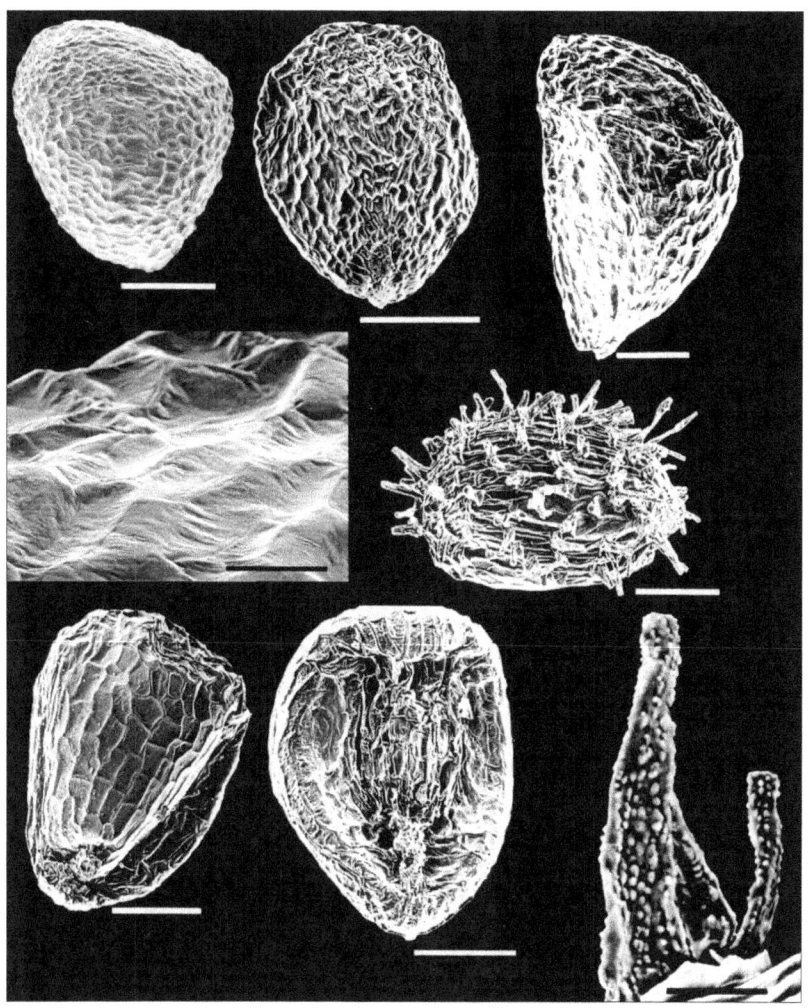

Figure 22. Seeds of the Lythraceae. Left-to-right, top-to-bottom: *Adenaria floribunda*. *Ammania coccinea* (middle-right, wetted seed with emergent epidermal cell trichomes). *A. erecta*. Epidermal cell trichomes of *A. coccinea*. S. Graham and A. Graham, 2014.

- In addition to such highly innovative ways of getting
  about, plants with no exceptional means of long-distance
  transport readily move around the world thanks to
  human activity both deliberate and accidental: carried
  unintentionally with soils, trade goods, and ship ballast, for
  example, as well as intentionally introduced in locations
  beyond the plant's own native range. Similarly, the seeds
  of such plants may be dispersed by hurricanes, as was
  probably the case with the European *Lythrum tribracteatum*
  (threebract loosestrife) now growing in the San Francisco
  Bay area of California and the Latin American *Cuphea
  glandulosa* in Mobile, Alabama. Numerous other seeds are
  continually being accidentally or purposefully introduced,
  after which they escape into the natural vegetation.

That is, by innumerable devices seeds get on and
inside things, animate and inanimate, living and dead.
The combination can tell if they came from a location
with natural vegetation like a forest or from a human-
made or modified assemblage such as a greenhouse,
garden, or weedy farmyard. They all have a tale to tell
about when and where, and who is telling the truth
and who is not. For example, Shirley Graham writes,

> In 1997 I was called by the sheriff's department
> of Champaign County near Columbus, Ohio, to
> identify some seeds associated with the murder
> of two children found buried at the shady
> wooded margin of a local cemetery not long after

they were reported missing by the stepfather. I identified the seeds as from *Geum canadense* (Rosaceae) and *Galium aparine* (Rubiaceae), species of shaded to partly sunny places in dry to moist somewhat disturbed woodlands. The seeds had been removed from a blanket and the stepfather's clothing recovered at his house. He claimed the seeds came from his small farmyard, but neither plant occurred in his open weedy yard. Both species were found at the gravesite. The seed evidence linked the suspect to a wooded area such as at the gravesite and was part of the evidence introduced at the trial. He was convicted of the two murders and is now serving two life sentences. (State v. Neal, 2002-Ohio-6786; S. Graham, 2006).

Trichomes

Trichomes (Figures 23 and 24) are small hairs that can occur in plants. They appear in a variety of forms: for example, scattered over the surface of a seed as mentioned for *Cuphea,* or arranged into dense mat-like coverings that function to reduce water loss and to protect the plant against infection and predators. Trichomes may be microscopic, simple in structure, single celled, unbranched, with a soft texture, smooth surface, and tapering to a pointed tip. In other instances they are large, multicellular, branched into stellate (radiating) or dendritic (branched) forms, and further modified into spines, scales, hairs, and glands like those that secrete the stinging histamines of *Urtica* (nettle), the digestive enzymes of the insectivorous *Drosera* (sundews) and *Dionaea* (Venus flytrap), and the essential oils of the mints and other aromatic herbs.

The diversity is often not enough to allow identification of detached trichomes to the level of genus or species. There are exceptions, like *Cannabis*, the trichomes of which produce its distinctive cannabinoids. The subject of *Cannabis* classification came to national attention when Richard Evans Schultes of Harvard University intimated that there may be more than one species (Schultes et al., 1974). Though the classification has settled out as three forms—C. sativa, C. indica, and the hybrid and possibly ancestral C. ruderalis—molecular studies have raised the possibility of an even more complex evolutionary history and the need for an expanded taxonomy.

American law as written prohibited the cultivation, use, and trade of only *C. sativa*. Crushed plant material could not readily be recognized to species by law enforcement agents; the distinction could only be made microscopically, by experts using epidermal cell and trichome features. Schultes and Ernest Small, a taxonomist with Agriculture and Agri-Food Canada, engaged in heated debates during this period and served as opposing expert witnesses in court cases. It was ruled that the intent of the law was not to decide taxonomy but rather to regulate the use of a hallucinogen, and all three *Cannabis* taxa contain various amounts of cannabinoids,

Figure 23. SEM of trichomes of *Sphaeralcea coccinea*. Bates et al., 1997.

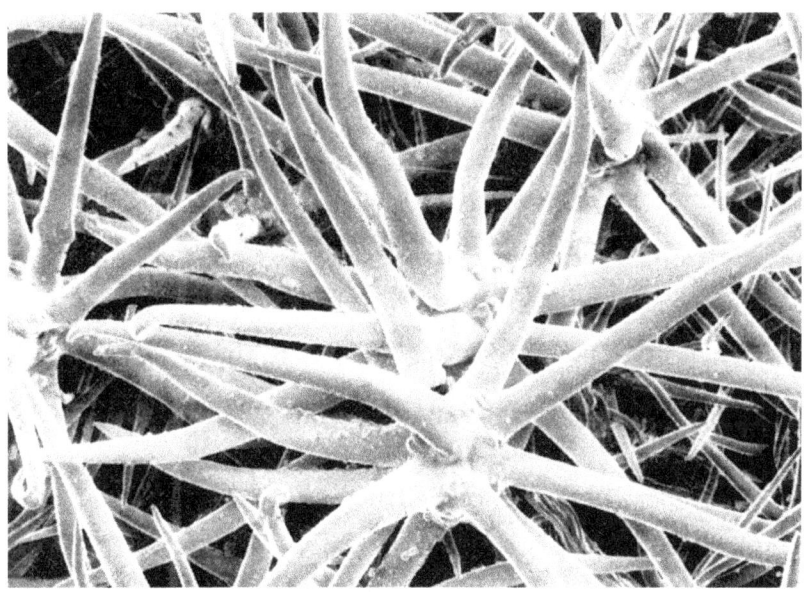

Figure 24. SEM of trichomes of *Sphaeralcea angustifolia*. Bates et al., 1997.

the plant's psychoactive compounds. The recent trend away from criminalizing the growing and use of marijuana (several companies cultivating cannabis and/or serving the cannabis industry are now listed on the New York Stock Exchange) has reduced the intensity of these arguments.

Trichomes have been reported from the Oligocene Baltic amber and are known as fossils and subfossils preserved as *compressions* (where the plant part is compacted between layers of sediment, as opposed to *impressions* where an imprint but little or no organic material remains). Trichomes can help verify extinctions through time; identify plants associated with or used by ancient cultures; determine the vegetation type, location, and season when an object or person was discarded; and ascertain whether a corpse or other remains have been moved or are still *in situ*.

Wood

As most schoolchildren learn, the alternating light and dark wood circles visible in the cross section of a tree trunk offer information about the tree's age and past growing conditions. While the principle behind this is simple, the science of dendrochronology, or tree ring analysis, is more complex.

Growth and the production of new cells in plants are confined to specific tissues called meristems.

- Apical meristems are located at the tips of stem branches and roots and are responsible for vertical growth. The tissue derived from apical meristems is called primary growth or tissue; plants composed mostly of primary tissue are typically annual in life span and herbaceous in texture (for example, herbs).

- The one-cell-layer-wide cylindrical column of cells that develop within the stem is called a lateral meristem or cambium and is responsible for a plant's increased girth. The tissue produced by the lateral meristem is called secondary growth or tissue. Lateral meristems are found in all woody plants and some herbaceous ones.

    Primary and secondary tissues include xylem and phloem.
- Xylem (wood) is composed of tracheids, specialized elongated cells used for transport, in all vascular plants; and vessels and fibers additionally in most angiosperms. Tracheids and vessels carry water and mineral nutrients up from the soil to the site of photosynthesis in the leaves, and fibers (as in flax) provide strength and support.

- Phloem (sieve tube elements and companion cells) carries the organic products of photosynthesis manufactured in the leaves down to storage areas in the stem and root. Much more secondary xylem is produced than secondary phloem so that about 90% of the cross-sectional area of a tree stem is wood (Figure 25).

During the spring of the year, when days are long, water plentiful, temperatures warm, and nutrients abundant, the xylem cells produced by the cambium are relatively large and numerous. They form broad, light colored bands called spring wood. Later in the summer and fall the wood cells become smaller and denser, forming a narrow dark ring until growth finally stops in the winter. The next spring, good (or at least better) growing conditions resume. The alternation of light spring wood against darker summer wood allows for easily countable annual growth rings (Figure 25).

In a living tree, the total number of rings tell the age of the tree. Since each ring is attributable to a single year, the width of the spring wood tells the approximate climate (good or bad) of that year, especially temperature and rainfall. Measured under control conditions of temperature and moisture, the width of the rings in living trees has been used to calibrate specific climate values. Because the lives of some trees are so lengthy, this helps create a record that spans millennia: in the western U.S. some trees of *Pinus aristata* (bristlecone pine) have lived for approximately 5,068 years and *Sequoia giganteum* for 3,266 years, while in the Eastern United States a *Taxodium ascendens* (cypress) tree grew for 3,500 years. The pattern of widths across a section can be matched between living trees, recently dead ones, subfossils in bogs and lakes, shoring timbers in archaeological structures and older fossils to give an annual record that extends back continuously for over 8,800 years and discontinuously for millions of years. Examined in the context of other information from soils, geology, geochemistry, and associated faunas now makes dendrochronology as precise a tool for identifying past climates as fingerprints are for ascertaining identity.

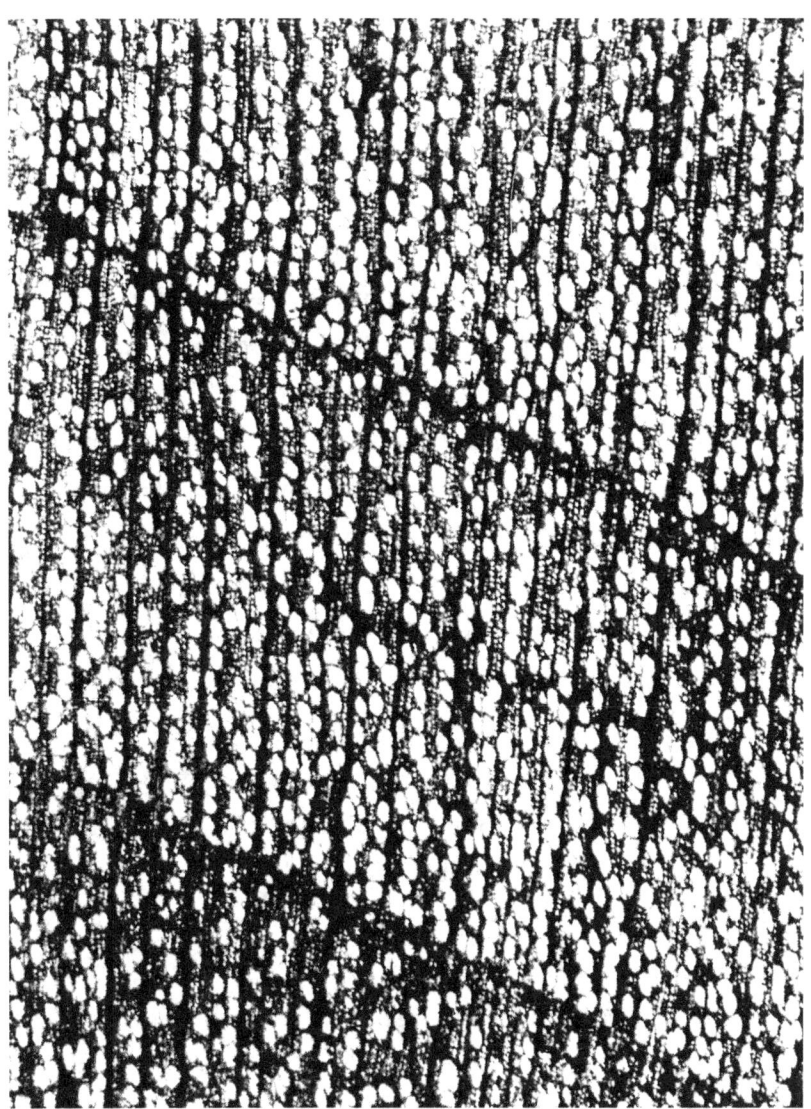

Figure 25. Cross-section through the secondary xylem of petrified wood of *Magnolia longiradiata* from the middle Eocene Clarno Formation, Oregon. Note the two horizontal growth rings indicating a seasonal climate and the vertical bands of small dark fibers (support) and larger open tracheids and vessels (conduction). Scott and Wheeler, 1982.

Dendrochronology has long been used for a variety of purposes such as dating the time of fires, floods, epidemics, earthquakes, landslides, land clearing, and agricultural activities around archaeological sites. These events leave their mark on plants down to a particular set of growth rings (year or years) so the time of the event often can be determined exactly. For example, in the days of early American land rushes, tree trunks were cut with slash marks to define the boundaries between acreages the government allotted. The scars on these marker trees eventually healed, and over the years the marker trees became difficult to recognize. Even then, however, they could be identified by felling trees or taking cores from the wood, from which the year the slash was cut could be accurately determined.

Its evidentiary use has brought dendrochronology not infrequently into the courtroom. One prominent example occurred in settling the boundary dispute between Texas and Oklahoma in a case argued before the U.S. Supreme Court in 1919. The original boundary was set as the mid-channel of the Red River, but Oklahoma argued that the river had gradually eroded northward to its expense and Texas's benefit. Early on, the exact position of the line was of no great importance. Then one of the largest oil fields in the world was discovered with the drilling of Spindletop near Beaumont, Texas on January 10, 1901. The Spindletop petroleum reservoir was huge: when it "blew" (Figure 26) the oil gushed for nine days at a rate of some 100,000 barrels a day. The Spindletop strike ushered the U.S. into the oil age, and every bit of land in its vicinity suddenly became immensely valuable.

Botanist Benjamin Carroll Tharp was a graduate student at the University of Texas at the time. Texas retained him as an expert witness for the defense. "Not being able to tell the age of a tree by looking at the bark," he said, Tharp had some trees on the disputed land felled. His analysis of their rings proved that thee trees had been growing continuously in the river's channel from long before the existing boundary had been established, and many of them were still there at the time of the trial in 1919 (Graham, 2010). There was no way the river could have eroded its way across the region leaving the trees standing. This information proved key in the Court's 1923 decision to leave the boundary as originally established.

Other cases demonstrate the applicability of dendrochronology to criminal investigations. Forensic botanist Jane Bock and environmental endocrinologist David Norris list several examples in their forensic plant science textbook (Bock and Norris 2016, chapter 5). The FBI's 2013 *Handbook of Forensic Services* notes that wood, cells such as flax and cotton fibers, and other plant material should be collected by the operatives processing crime scenes and submitted for expert examination. In this way, one of the world's most sophisticated investigatory bodies affirms the value of plant evidence in solving, or at least illuminating, complex events and crimes.

Figure 26. Spindletop gusher, south of Beaumont, Texas, 1901 January. Photograph by John Trost courtesy of Wikipedia.

THE REAL DEAL

The uses to which plant evidence can be put are as many
and complex as the plant components described above.
No single case, inquiry or event demonstrates all or even
most of these possibilities. Turning from plants themselves
to puzzles involving them, we look at four investigations
in which plant material played a significant role. Strikingly
different in purpose, players, stakes and scope, all nevertheless
highlight the roles that small botanical fragments can play
in answering large and figuratively thorny questions.

SCIENTIFIC INVESTIGATIONS

The first two of the four real-life investigations that are
described below address questions of history and science.

Mass extinctions through geologic time

Current science places the origin of time (and ultimately
everything else) at the "big bang" approximately 14 billion
years ago. There was subsequent differentiation of the

universes or galaxies (such as our Milky Way) and their component solar systems of stars (our Sun) and rotating planets (such as Earth) and moons. Estimates place Earth's origin at about 4.5 billion years ago with the formation of the first slag constituting a solidifying surface.

Initially, the planet was under physical and chemical not biological control. Then life appeared about 3.7 billion years ago, as evidenced by the first known fossils in rocks now scattered in places like Greenland, Australia, and at the base of the Grand Canyon, Arizona (Allenwood et al., 2018; Nutman et al., 2016; Van Zuillen, 2018). Approximately 635 million years ago in the late pre-Cambrian and early Cambrian Periods the planet saw an explosive differentiation of life, facilitated by the rise to prominence of self-sustaining photosynthetic marine blue-green algae that served as a food source for other non-photosynthesizing organisms.

Scientists now date what they call the "move to the land" to the early part of the Middle Ordovician Period approximately 475 million years ago. The supply of oxygen evaporating from the ocean to the atmosphere made the transition possible at that time (Taylor et al., 2009). The first animals, dependent on plants for oxygen and ultimately for nutrients, likely appeared about 425 million years ago. From that point, Earth's biota was repeatedly transformed as changes in its environment caused mass extinctions and diversification among organisms (Hallam and Wignall, 1997) and the race was on. A new kind of flora appeared after each disruption, followed soon (in geological terms) by a new fauna. Five such mass extinction events have occurred on Earth to date.

The first mass extinction happened near the transition from the Ordovician to the Silurian Periods some 440 million years ago, prior to the appearance of any extensive land flora. It affected the marine fauna of the time including the trilobites, brachiopods, graptolites, and the early blue-green algae. Causes of this extinction included the planet's cooling to the point of glaciation, an associated sea-level decline resulting in changes to the ocean's chemical composition, and extensive volcanic activity that furthered the lowering of atmospheric CO_2 concentration. In the late Ordovician Period, however, marine calcareous green algae (Chlorophyta) such as *Ischadites* (Kesling and Graham, 1962) appeared. The Chlorophyta gave rise to, and share several features with, the land-based vascular plants (those with xylem and phloem) we recognize today, and hence form a key evolutionary stepping stone.

By the time the second major extinction event took place in the late Devonian Period some 365 million years ago, the vascular flora growing on land was becoming diverse and widespread. Some plants were cryptogamous (without seeds), but others included the very earliest seed plants. Among the latter were the pteridosperms or seed ferns, extinct fernlike plants that included *Archaeospermum arnoldii* from Pennsylvania (Pettitt and Beck, 1968) and *Elkinsia polymorpha* from West Virginia (Rothwell et al., 1989). The earliest of the vascular plants, along with some seed ferns, survived to the end or possibly just after the beginning of the Cretaceous period. The reason(s) for the mass extinction at the end of the Devonian Period are poorly known, but the event seems attributed to multiple causes: anoxia (depletion of dissolved oxygen in the ocean waters), climate change as evidenced by glaciation, and a corresponding drop in sea level. It has been suggested that with the rise of land plants there was an increase in the amount of organic debris transported into the ocean, which reduced oxygen as it decayed (Algeo et al., 1995; see also Algeeo and Scheckler, 1998; Algeo, Schleckler, and Maynard, 2000; McGhee, 1996; Streel et al., 2000). Whatever the cause, some 20% of the animal families became extinct. The event had a less dramatic effect on plants, but some 80% of Earth's then-existing species vanished.

At the beginning of the Permian period, about 290 million years ago, a third major change in climate took place. With great aridity evidenced by widespread occurrence of evaporite (salt and mineral) deposits, the "great dying" saw 96% of all terrestrial species become extinct. Organisms able to transport and conserve water efficiently survived and succeeded. These included the gymnosperms and reptiles, prominent among which were the dinosaurs. The age of the gymnosperms and dinosaurs lasted through the Triassic and Jurassic Periods, for approximately 108 million years.

Toward the end of the Jurassic and into the early Cretaceous Periods 150 to 140 million years ago, continental drift and more equable climates brought more of the Earth's biota into environments characterized by a moderate amount of moisture. The angiosperms appeared during this time, for reasons that were not clear to Charles Darwin (who called this an "abominable mystery") or to scientists today. The oldest widely accepted angiosperm fossils date to the early to mid-Cretaceous Period about 135-134 million years ago. Competition arose between the older, drier-habitat gymnosperms and the emerging angiosperms. The latter had several advantages. As noted earlier, angiosperm seeds are enclosed by both a protective seed coat (like that of the gymnosperms) but also by a nutritive fruit. The vessels and fibers in the xylem, in addition to their tracheids, made for better transport and strength; their flowers could be pollinated and the subsequent seeds dispersed more widely by the methods described above. In a sense, in the early and middle Cretaceous years the stage was set for any event that would tip the balance from gymnosperms to angiosperms and from reptiles to other groups of animals.

That fifth and deciding event came at the end of the Cretaceous era, approximately 65 million years ago. The demise of the dinosaurs at that time is familiar, even to children, from a wealth of scientific information, television specials, fiction and documentary films, and even cartoons. In one of the latter, a generically sketched *Brontosaurus* is discussing investments with a stockbroker. Looking at brochures on plastics and fossil fuels, it says, "I don't care how they are made as long as they pay dividends."

The dinosaurs' crash was the result of a meteorite landing on the Yucatán Peninsula of Mexico. Approximately

ten kilometers (seven miles) in diameter, it hit land with
an impact estimated to be ten times that of the world's
nuclear arsenal and left a crater 180 kilometers—about
120 miles—wide. Great near-global wildfires provided
new habitats for invasion and smoke and dust abruptly if
temporarily lowered temperatures in a climate that had
already begun to cool in the middle Cretaceous. As is
frequently true, some species found the cataclysm to their
benefit. The subsequent diversification and co-evolution
of insects and other animals further enhanced dispersal
and pollination in the angiosperms. Among animal groups,
the therapsid reptiles, unique in having legs that were
located directly under the body rather than along the side,
coped particularly well. The therapsid-derived mammals
later gave rise to the hominids, a group that includes the
great apes, chimpanzees, orangutans, and early humans.

Depending on how one defines the term, early members
of the hominid line appear around the middle Miocene era
approximately nine million years ago. Human-like apes split
from chimpanzees circa 5 to 6 million years ago. *Ardipithecus*,
the earliest biped, appears at approximately 4 million years
ago, *Australopithecus afarensis* (which moved in an upright
walking gait) 3.2 million years ago, and early use of natural
tools—and possibly early tool producers—about 2.6 million
years ago. Semi-controlled use of fire was first seen 300,000
years ago; *Homo sapiens* appeared approximately 100,000
year later and its first use of something that qualifies as a
language 20,000 years after that. Evidence from fossilized

pollen (Iversen, 1949, 1956) indicates that agriculture was first seen approximately 12,000 years ago in the Middle East but then moved northward, toward northwest Europe, from the vicinity of the Tigris/Euphrates River. At least in Africa and western Europe, humans began writing some 6,000 years ago.

Though obviously disastrous to the species involved, these five mass extinctions were a major force in the evolution of new and improved species and communities. A number of contemporary scientists today point to the degradation of key habitats such as rainforests and coral reefs, as well as the disappearance of many flora and fauna families, as evidence that a sixth one is underway or at least imminent. Unlike its earlier equivalents, extinction will be driven by human activity and human destruction of the flora will feature prominently in the change. The outcome cannot be foreseen but a growing consensus is that it may not be survivable.

Humanity of the Neanderthals: How far did they go?

For the past 65,000 years, the dark opening to Shanidar Cave on the side of Bradost Mountain in the Zagros Range of northern Iraq has been an inviting place to hide things for safe keeping. Among the most important things ever hidden there were the bodies of ten Neanderthals (*Homo neanderthalensis*). Their burial took place some 56,000 years ago.

The bones are preserved in a Mousterian or Mode III layer named after the type site at Le Moustier in France. It is defined as a zone containing stone tools of the earliest anatomically modern humans for any given region. In Western

Eurasia this was at the end of the middle Paleolithic or Old Stone Age and extends from ca. 315,000 to 35,000-30,000 BP. The tools are smaller and sharper than older ones suggesting the Neanderthals were more dexterous and had a stronger grip than their predecessors. In Israel and elsewhere Neanderthals, *Homo sapiens*, and Mousterian tools have been found in association (Levy, 2001) so they were together at several places at the same time.

The oldest known Neanderthals lived in Europe approximately 430,000 years ago. From there, they radiated into central Europe and central and eastern Asia. *H. sapiens* appeared in northeast Africa some 300,000 years ago and moved into Asia approximately 100,000 years ago. The paths of the two crossed several times at different places, and in one area—northern Mongolia and Siberia—also met up with another species of humans called the Denisovans (*H. sapiens denisova*).

We know a lot about the Neanderthals physically. They were quite modern looking: if you passed one on most city streets today, you probably wouldn't even notice. The adults were stocky and muscular, roughly 5'4" in height and 170 pounds in weight. They had a maximum life span of approximately 50 years, equivalent to about 80 years today. Their cranial capacity (1133.98 cubic centimeters) was about the same as that of *H. sapiens* (1332.41 cubic centimeters). The differences in physical and psychological characteristics between the two species are due not so much to brain size but to the proportion of the lobes devoted to various tasks. In the Neanderthals the visual cortex, concerned with vision and muscular development, was larger; in Sapiens, the parietal lobe was more extensively developed. The latter deals with cognition—that is, with acquiring and storing knowledge, formulating myths, planning, and anticipating. These capacities continued (and continue) to expand through experience and thought but they began from a larger base and reached more complex levels in Sapiens.

Our interest here, however, is not so much in what the Shanidar Neanderthals were like physically. Rather, the question is whether they were behaviorally and culturally human as well. It is a fascinating question, which plant evidence helps to answer.

Aspects of the Shanidar Cave burial feel distinctly human in modern terms. The Neanderthals seem to have lowered the body of their companions carefully onto the floor of the cave that would be their final resting place. The ceremony included pre-burial preparations, with flowers placed on the floor of the grave and alongside the bodies. The presence of this plant material has been interpreted to show *Homo neanderthalensis* had a concern for the remains of the dead, an interpretation that went a long way in supporting the view they were comparable in spirit and behavior as well as physical form to modern *Homo sapiens*. Or did it? Would this particular piece of evidence hold up under closer examination?

The Neanderthal bodies at Shanidar were unearthed in 1957 and the results published by Crubézy and Trinkaus (1992), Solecki (1975), Stewart (1959), Trinkaus (1983), and others. Four of the ten bodies were particularly rich in evidence about what they experienced while alive and how they coped with the life they were dealt.

The man known to science as Shanidar I lived to about 50 years of age. This was unusual, being at the far end of Neanderthal life span. It was even more remarkable because of the severe abnormalities he suffered. Shanidar I had a withered right arm, which was fractured in several places and caused the loss of use of the lower arm and hand, which were eventually amputated. Analysis also indicates that his legs and feet were paralyzed. He was blind in one eye and suffered a severe hearing loss as a result of "a violent blow to the left side of his face, creating a crushing fracture to his left orbit."[4] In other words, as would be expected, accidental and deliberate injuries occurred among the early humans. Shanidar I was debilitated by congenital defects and later by accident or abuse, but he was also cared for over a long period of time by others attentive to his welfare.

It is interesting to compare his condition with that of another body found along the River Irtysh on the plains of Siberian Russia dated by molecular means to ca. 45,000 years ago. This individual was unlike Shanidar I, who had physical defects but was still cared for. "The young man slowly crept down the gravel gulch in the dawn of remote Russia keeping his eyes keenly fixed on his prey. There were many animals about but he was tracking one in particular. It was a lone elephant-like beast with large curved tusks, patches of matted hair over its body, and relatively small in size. Suddenly a crushing blow came down violently on the young man's skull and he was a predator no more" (Graham, in prep).

The second Neanderthal body, Shanidar 2, died in a rock fall and, like Shanidar 1, was given a ritual burial. Also like Shanidar 1, he was elderly by Neanderthal standards at the time of his death. He was honored with worked stones and a fire built alongside his final resting place. Shanidar 3 died from a stab wound; it is not clear whether the injury was accidental or purposeful, but its position and angle of entry indicate that it was not self-inflicted. The wound came from a pointed missile presumably hurled from a projectile device and, if purposeful, indicates conflict within the Neanderthals or between them and the Sapiens in the area. Either way the event is telling, because it is the only known example of violence involving the Neanderthals. (Other incidences of violence must have happened, but they were not common.) The healing pattern indicates that Shanidar 3 lived for several weeks after his wounding and must have been provided with food, water, and protection by those who cared.

From the standpoint of botanical evidence, the clues offered by the body of Shanidar 4 are both the most informative and the most complicated. Roughly 45 years old at death, he was laid to rest on his left side in the fetal position as was common at the time. Soil samples recently taken from alongside the body have been used to reconstruct the setting and events at the time of burial. Two of these samples contained clumps of 100 or more pollen grains, which have been interpreted as likely having come from clusters of flowers. Some of the grains even retain the elongated shape of the anthers in which they were once contained. Further suggesting the plants were insect-pollinated rather than wind pollinated and brought into the cave, one of the samples contained a butterfly wing. Among the angiosperm pollen types recovered were *Achillea, Senecio, Centaurea*, and *Muscaria*, all of which have conspicuous flowers and grow in the vicinity of the cave today. The many grains of *Althaea* (Malvaceae) pollen were particularly noteworthy. Large and sticky, this pollen further indicates transport into the cave by means other than wind.

Several of the plants just mentioned have medicinal properties. One plausible explanation was that Shanidar 4 was a shaman or healer and the plants placed beside him were part of a ritual burial (Leroi-Gourhan, 1975), a uniquely human practice. It may be speculated that because Shanidar 1 and 3 were advanced in years they, too, served some kind of shamanistic role. However, if Shanidar 2 and 4 were not shamans they were unusually old and received similar attention.

The intriguing aspects of Shanidar 4's burial have led to exuberant interpretation. For example, Ralph S. Solecki's *Shanidar, The First Flower People* notes that "With the finding of flowers in association with Neanderthals, we are brought suddenly to the realization that the universality of mankind and the love of beauty go beyond the boundary of our own species. No longer can we deny the early men the full range of human feelings and experience" (Solecki, 1971).

However, problems soon arose with such conclusions. Later research discovered a small local rodent called the Persian jird, a gerbil-like creature that gathers plant material and stores it in burrows. The activities of this rodent, still found in and around the Shanidar cave today, (Sommer, 1999) may explain the presence of ancient plant material in the cave more convincingly than assumptions of human introduction. Further, though the *Althaea* grains seem unlikely to have been transported by air, most of the other pollen was found in similar concentrations inside and outside the cave, suggesting that wind was a factor. A new consensus, presented with some certainty and finality of its own, is that "… the deliberate placement of flowers has been convincingly eliminated" (Pettitt, 2002, p. 8). This has opened the way for interpretation of Neanderthal humanity colored by a very different agenda. For example, a 2015 article in the British periodical *The Telegraph* asserts that "Instead of viewing hominids as evolutionary intermediates, our biblically based human origins model regards hominids, such as Neanderthals, as *animals* made by God with limited emotional and intellectual capacities. The biological similarities between humans and hominids are a manifestation of common design, not common descent. Modern humans …uniquely possess the capacity for symbolism and, consequently, the capacity for language, art, and music. Furthermore, modern humans are the only creatures that engage in religious practices" (Douglas, 2015).

The placement of flowers at grave sites by Neanderthals, especially later in their history after long and intimate contact with *H. sapiens*, may now have "come under scrutiny," (Stromberg, 2013) but it has not been convincingly "eliminated." A third and more moderate view posits that "at least some Neanderthals, at some times, treated the dead body…and indulged in primary corpse modification and subsequent burial…and that their function as such was perpetuated in the memory of Neanderthal groups either through physical grave markers or social tradition. In all, it would seem that at least in some Neanderthal groups the dead body was explored and treated in socially meaningful ways" (Stromberg, 2013, p. 1).

Ultimately, the consensus on the question of whether the Neanderthals placed and arranged flowers under or alongside their dead, first based on botanical evidence and then on reexamination of that evidence, is that they probably did not. In other ways, however—the care and treatment of the dead body, the observance of burial rituals, the use of grave markers, and the willingness to care for the injured—they did exhibit human feelings.

Cohabiting, interacting, and interbreeding with the Neanderthals at the very end of the latter's existence some 30,000 years ago, *H. sapiens* seems to have served as mentors of sorts. They likely exposed the Neanderthals to the use of plants for both health care and ceremony as well as introducing other customs. One was use of art, in the form of sculptures and drawings, to express feelings and beliefs. Early inhabitants of the Siberian region prior to about 40, 000 years ago likely arranged stones into pyramidal clusters, spires, and circles to house the sprits and protect those coming to honor them.

A little later in time, such structures have been found adorned with the carvings known as petroglyphs. Until recently the oldest known of these was a human handprint approximately 30,000 years old from Chauvet-Pont-d'Arc Cave in southern France. Other examples are from Winnemucca Lake, Nevada (14,800 - 10,500 years old); Atltai, Siberia (12,000 - 10,000 years old); and over 1,200 stone carvings among the spires and circles of what is now known as Petroglyph Park, Petrozavodsk, Lake Onega, NW Russia (approximately 4,000 years old). Since the Altai Mountain region yielded DNA of inhabitants living there only 45,000 and 41,000 years ago, it was expected that older petroglyphs would likely be found there or elsewhere. Most recently, an abstract cross-hatched design 73,000 years old has been found on a rock flake in Blombos Cave in southern South Africa (Henshilwood et al., 2018). It was examined with "forensic thoroughness" (Nature, 2018, p. 149) and appears to have been drawn using a crayon-like object of red ochre; i.e., a painting as opposed to an engraving like ones known 540,000 years ago on shells from Java and presumably done by *H. erectus*. Cave paintings about 64,000 years old in Spain have been directly attributed to the Neanderthals (Hoffmann et al., 2018), as have such paintings from 40,000 years ago in Indonesia (Aubert, 2014). The latter includes 12 human hand stencils and two figurative animal depictions from seven cave sites and establishes artwork "at opposite

ends of the Pleistocene Eurasian world" (p. 223). As all
of this demonstrates, art was being used "worldwide to
express sympathy, pride, joy and other emotions. These
findings suggest…it was ubiquitous through time, tying us
to those who lived many millennia ago" (Stromberg, 2013,
p. 3). In *The Smart Neanderthal: Bird Catching, Cave Art, and
the Cognitive Revolution*, Clive Finlayson argues that "our
nearest cousins were our cognitive equals" (Wood, 2019).

Though it occurred well beyond the demise of the
Neanderthals at about 30,000 years ago, the recent
discovery of flowers buried in a 12,000-year-old cemetery
in Israel (Nadel et al., 2013) affirms again the relevance
of plant material to the assessment of our ancestors'
natures, consciousness and capacities. Plant impressions
and phytoliths were discovered beneath two bodies at
a site set aside especially for burials. Laid out straight
rather than in the fetal position more common in
earlier burials, the bodies were decorated with beads,
pigments, and flowers from plants including *Salvia judaica*
(sage), members of the Scrophulariaceae (figwort), and
possibly *Cercis siliquastrum* (Judas tree), among others.
The blossoms were interwoven into a mat on which the
bodies were placed. Such complex arrangements could
not have arisen in full-blown form. Instead, they suggest
that simpler use of plant material in burial ritual must
have begun at some as yet unknown earlier date.

Even based on the documented evidence discussed
above, the Neanderthals had numerous traits—care for the

injured and weak, attention to the remains of the dead, and observance of burial rituals—that we not only recognize as fundamentally human but also admire. They further developed other behaviors, such as the making of art, which we view as enriching human life, connections and communities. Thus, to the "accusation" of humanity, behaviorally as well as physically, the Neanderthals must be found guilty as charged—and plant investigative material played a key role in the verdict.

FORENSIC INVESTIGATIONS

While the word "forensic" is now most commonly used in the context of crimes, its earlier meaning, derived from its Latin source, was the more general "related to courts of law." That is, forensic investigations involve the legal system in some way, rather than necessarily focusing on criminal charges. The two cases discussed below reflect that broader definition, exploring the equally significant role plant material played in the resolution of one criminal and one civil case.

"*Homo sapiens* holds the record among all organisms for driving the most plant and animal species to extinctions," writes historian and philosopher Yuval Noah Harari in his 2015 book *Sapiens: A Brief History of Mankind*, adding, "We have the dubious distinction of being the deadliest species in the annals of biology" (p. 74). Affirming this conclusion, each and every hundred years offers us numerous contenders for the title "crime of the century," whether we measure the acts by their brutality, media attention, public reaction, or impact on subsequent history.

Certainly, the nineteenth century has a likely winner. One of the most notorious crimes in history was the murder and dismemberment of 11 persons, mostly female, poor, and pursuing some form of prostitution, in the Whitechapel district of London in 1888. Five of the killings took place between August 31 and November 9 of that year and were attributed to the serial killer known as Jack the Ripper. Considerable misinformation surrounded the crimes, which generated a number of subsequent copycat murders. The impact on polite society was muted by the facts that the victims were portrayed as living at the edge of morality and potentially related crimes extended through 1891. The killer was never caught, and extensive analysis of the crimes over the years in both scholarly and popular publications has produced controversial hypotheses but no consensus on the identity of the killer.

In the next century, the shock of a later killing was augmented by its suddenness and by the fact the victim lived at the apex of power, wealth, and public importance. At one moment on November 22, 1963, John F. Kennedy was alive; seconds later, he was dead. Lee Harvey Oswald loaded his rifle on the sixth floor of the Texas School Book Depository and at 12:30 p.m. ended the dream of an American Camelot. The shock was intense and immediate but the effects were enduring. Coupled with events including America's deepening engagement in a war in Vietnam perceived by many to be illegitimate, flaws in the investigation of the Kennedy assassination among other factors helped make an increasing segment of the nation's people less willing to accept the authority of government and law enforcement, particularly when regulators do not abide by the rules themselves.

The Lindbergh Baby Kidnapping

Significant as Kennedy's assassination was in historical terms another crime was touted as the "crime of the century." Whether or not one agrees, the designation was well-earned: it involved the private life of a national hero, it targeted a child, and its investigation was full of unexpected twists.

A handsome, 25-year old airmail pilot, Charles Lindbergh gained fame as the first person to fly solo, non-stop across the Atlantic Ocean in a flight from Roosevelt Field in New York to Paris in May 1927. He married Anne Morrow, daughter of U.S. Ambassador to Mexico Dwight Morrow, in 1929 and their first son, Charles Lindbergh, Jr. was born the following year.

On the night of March 1, 1932, the child was kidnapped from his second-story nursery at their home in Hopewell, New Jersey. The kidnapper propped a homemade ladder against the side of the house (Figure 27) and left a ransom note on the windowsill. Lindbergh's fame drew the attention of media nationwide, and the pilot himself as well as local and state police, military colonels helping as volunteers, and even figures from organized crime became involved in the investigation. After the receipt of additional ransom notes, arrangements were made for meeting with the kidnapper or possibly his representative (an adult male

Figure 27. The Lindbergh home at Hopewell, New Jersey showing the ladder to the second story window used in the kidnapping. S. Graham, 1997 (and sources credited therein).

with a German accent) on April 2, 1932 in the Woodlawn Cemetery, Bronx, New York. A ransom of $50,000 was later paid at the St. Raymond's cemetery based on the promise that instructions for finding the child would be forthcoming. The promise proved false, and the child's body was found on May 12 only a few miles from the Lindbergh home.

The investigation foundered for some time, but the ladder proved a crucial piece of evidence. Four kinds of wood were used in its construction: ponderosa pine (*Pinus ponderosa*), yellow pine (*Pinus* group), Douglas fir (*Pseudotsuga mensiesii*), and birch (cf. *Betula alba*). The year after the crime, microscopic analysis of ladder samples allowed detailed observation of the growth rings, knots, and tool marks in its wood. The ladder was simple but professionally made. Square nail holes not associated with its construction suggested that its wood had been used previously for some other purpose, while the absence of rust around the holes indicated that the wood had been used for something indoors. The tapering of the side rails and rungs together with the tool marks showed the wood came from a single strip, probably about 14 feet long and machined-dressed to 3 3/4 inches instead of the usual 3 5/8 inch measurement. The combination of the kind of wood used, its unusual dressing, and indications that the wood had been planed with a nicked blade led investigators to the Dorn Mill in McCormic, South Carolina, where the wood had been finished, and to the outlet store to which it had been shipped, the National Lumber and Millwork Company in Bronx, New York. However, authorities still knew only that they were looking for a carpenter with a German accent who likely lived in the Bronx.

Then bills with the serial numbers of the ransom money began to circulate. In September 1934, a gas station attendant recorded the license plate of a man who paid with one of the bills. Bruno Richard Hauptmann, a German carpenter living in the Bronx and owner of the car identified at the gas station, was arrested on September 19, 1934.

Hauptmann had previously been employed at the National Lumber and Millwork Company. Part of the ransom money was found in his attic. A search revealed a floorboard of yellow pine eight feet shorter than the others because its end piece had been sawed away. The four square nail holes in the side rail of the ladder matched holes in the remaining floorboard. Building on the earlier analyses of the ladder's wood, comparisons now showed that the width, number, and spacing of growth rings in the ladder rails and floorboard corresponded exactly, including a 1 3/8 inch gap cut to make the length of the rails match (Figure 28).

Held at New Jersey's Hunterdon County Courthouse and packed with luminaries including Damon Runyan, Jack Benny and Walter Winchell, the "trial of the century" commenced on January 2, 1935. Presentation of the plant evidence was made by Arthur Koehler, the chief wood technologist at the national research laboratory of the U.S. Forest Service. He spoke as the prosecution's last witness in testimony that has been called "elegant and convincing" (Baden, 1983) and "outstanding for its thoroughness and simplicity" (Tanay,

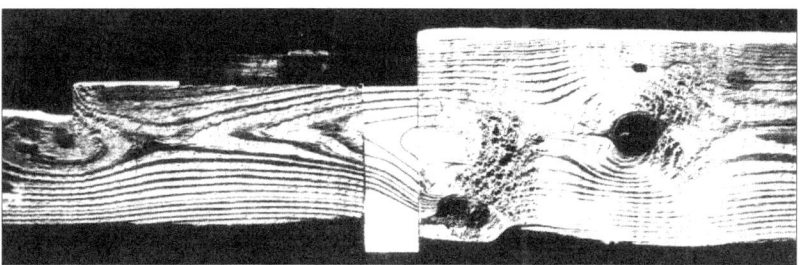

Figure 28. Portion of the side-rail (left) and floorboard from the Hauptmann attic (right) showing match of the growth rings. The insertion was added to demonstrate correspondence of the growth rings across a gap where a section was cut to even the length of the side-rails. S. Graham, 1997 (and sources credited therein).

1983). After a 32-day trial and fewer than twelve hours of jury deliberation, Hauptmann was convicted of murder in the first degree and subsequently executed on April 3, 1936.

As expected in such a high-profile case (and has also been true of the Ripper murders and the Kennedy assassination), fame and fortune was to be made from both claims and counterclaims about Hauptmann's guilt in the decades since the trial. The consensus, however, remains that there is little doubt about his guilt. The Lindberg case spurred the nation's first federal kidnapping law. More importantly for our purposes here, it was a turning point in the recognition of plant material as valid evidence and plant scientists as expert witnesses in criminal proceedings (S. Graham, 1997).

The Ruidoso Plane Crash

Not all, or even perhaps most, of the lawsuits filed against large corporations for negligence are filed with the expectation of going to trial. Plaintiffs may be ready from the start to accept less than the damages claimed in the suit in lieu of going to trial. Large corporations, which face these situations frequently, must decide if the expense of the settlement in time, money, and publicity is greater or less than the cost of litigation. From their point of view, payment may constitute only "nuisance money," unfortunate but essentially just one of the costs of doing business. In other cases, the sum involved is deemed excessive and the defendant decides to go to trial. This was the situation when

AlliedSignal, Beech Aircraft, and Pratt and Whitney were sued on behalf of a family whose parents were killed in a plane crash near Ruidoso, New Mexico on December 2, 1989.

The plane that crashed was a twin-engine Beechcraft Super King Air F90 equipped with two Pratt and Whitney engines. It left San Diego, California and flew to Sand Springs, Montana before heading south to Ruidoso, in the Sierra Blanca mountain range. Its pilot had less than 600 total hours of flying experience and less than 100 hours in this particular plane. The weather was bad on the day of the flight, with a cloud ceiling of 800 feet, visibility of less than 100 miles, and a snowfall underway. Later, defense attorney Stephen K. Brunk (Brunk, 1997, p. 378) noted that "the instrument approach to Ruidoso is a difficult one, and the system in use was a non-directional beacon (NDB), which is a somewhat archaic type of navigational aid." After the NDB was lost during the flight, the plane was heard flying off course above the clouds. Suddenly it emerged at full power from the clouds heading straight down and crashed in the mountains outside Ruidoso.

Later, a team of expert witnesses for the defense visited the scene. Three perfectly circular indentations made by the nose of the plane and both of its engines were clearly visible. There was no slant or angle, confirming that the plane had come straight down at full speed. It was difficult to avoid the conclusion that the pilot thought he was flying horizontally, when in fact he was heading vertically down.

The engines were sent to the Pratt and Whitney facilities in Montreal where they were disassembled and examined

under the supervision of the National Transportation and
Safety Board (NASB). Examination found nothing unusual
mechanically, nor anything that would have clogged or
otherwise interfered with the fuel transporting components.
In the spring of 1990 the engines were sent back to the
Ruidoso airport and dumped in an outdoor storage facility.
They remained there through the summer of 1990.

Then, attorneys representing the family examined the
wreckage. In one of the engines, they found what later
came to be a key piece of evidence. The B2 elbow is a
tubular part of the fuel control unit (FCU) that operates by
drawing air from outside the plane to regulate the supply
of fuel to the engine. In the elbow, they found a small
clump of vegetation and other debris that, if present during
operation of the plane, would have seriously impaired its
function. The contention was that the bend or elbow in
the tube was a design flaw resulting in accumulation of
debris from the outside air and caused the plane to crash.

That seemed unlikely for several reasons. Anything
getting into the unit would have to pass through a series of
compressor blades rotating at thousands of revolutions per
minute, which would pulverize any contaminant into powder.
Also, the temperature within the component is approximately
260° C (500° F), which the post-crash fire would have raised
to approximately 1000° C, incinerating any organic material.

The location of the plant and other debris also seemed
telling. Rather than being lodged in the bend of the
B2 elbow, it was found in an adjacent straight portion.

Similar matter was found in another part of the FCU that carried only fuel and not air from the outside. The pressure in the elbow—approximately 300 pounds per square inch, or ten times the pressure in an automobile tire—would likely have either prevented the accumulation, or dislodged any clump of organic matter in the tube.

Nonetheless, a suit was filed and the companies decided a defense would be made. The defense assembled a team of scientists and charged them with the task of establishing the nature of the organic mass and providing an explanation for its presence in the line. The full application of complex and highly technical evidence in investigative and court proceedings is usually constrained by cost considerations. Unusually, in this instance no limits were placed on the budget and the scientific team was able to make use of technologies including LM, SEM, TEM, Fournier Transform Infrared Spectroscopy Analysis (FTIR), and Energy Dispersive X-Ray Analysis (EDAX), putting interactive botanical and other forensic work on full display (Brunk, 1997, p. 379).

The results illuminate the ways in which precise analyses of plant materials—including such components as pollen, spores, and trichomes, discussed above—can help reconstruct or, conversely, debunk a proposed reconstruction of a disputed event.

Pollen and spores. When the debris from the B2 elbow was examined using LM, SEM, and TEM, a large part of the organic matter was found to consist of pollen. The pollen was glistening, bright yellow in color, and surrounded by a moist, sticky, hyaline substance that held the grains together in clumps. This suggested the pollen was fresh and probably still living at the time of examination. Germination experiments were conducted to determine if the pollen was, in fact, still viable. When placed in 10% sucrose solution, pollen tubes began to emerge from the pores (Figure 29), indicating that the protoplasm was intact. Recall that the heat and pressure levels inside the elbow while the plane was operating prior to the crash were very high, and that the wreckage was exposed to a post-crash fire so hot it melted aluminum and resin/fiberglass parts. Reference material from living plants growing immediately adjacent to the storage yard was processed to identify the pollen in the elbow (Figures 30 and 31).

The pollen found and studied was almost exclusively that of insect-pollinated rather than wind-pollinated plants. As noted earlier, this pollen is comparatively large, often spiny and/or sticky, allowing it to adhere to the pollinating vector (in situations like this, usually insects), and produced in relatively small quantities because pollination is relatively efficient. This is in contrast to wind-pollinated plants where the pollen as mentioned earlier is smaller, dry, smooth-surfaced, easily transportable, and produced in prodigious quantities since its landing on the female part of the flower occurs by random chance. Both insect- and wind-pollinated species grow in and around the storage yard, and as noted by Lewis (1997, p. 387), "There is no known mechanism whereby insect-pollinated types could selectively have been filtered from the air at the exclusion of the predominant wind-

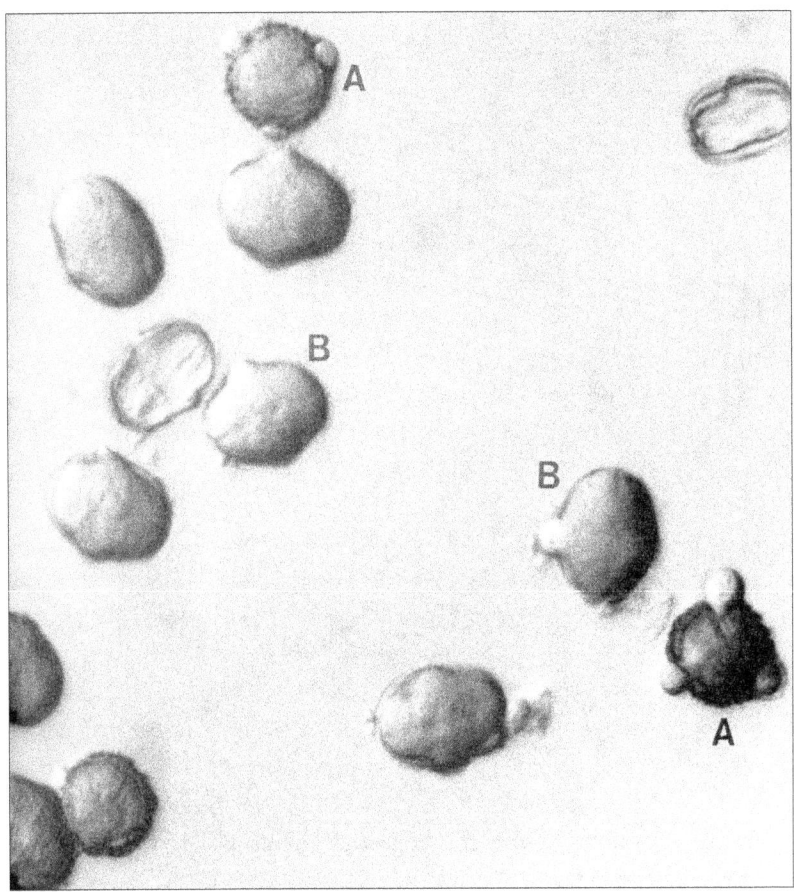

Figure 29. Germinating pollen (protrusion of pollen tubes from the apertures of *Grindelia squarrosa* (A) and *Melilotus officinalis* (B) in 10% sucrose solution. The pollen was taken from the B2 elbow of the wreckage and germination indicates it was living and the protoplasm intact. From Lewis, 1997.

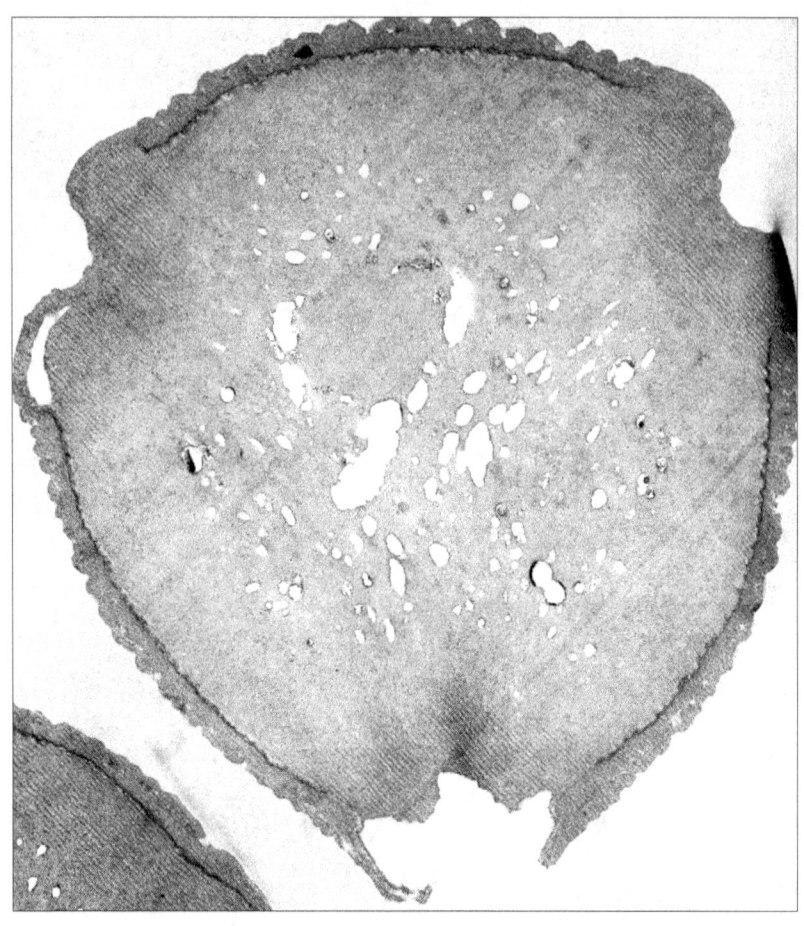

Figure 30. TEM section of *Meliotus officinalis* pollen from the storage yard. cf. with Figure 31. Lewis, 1997.

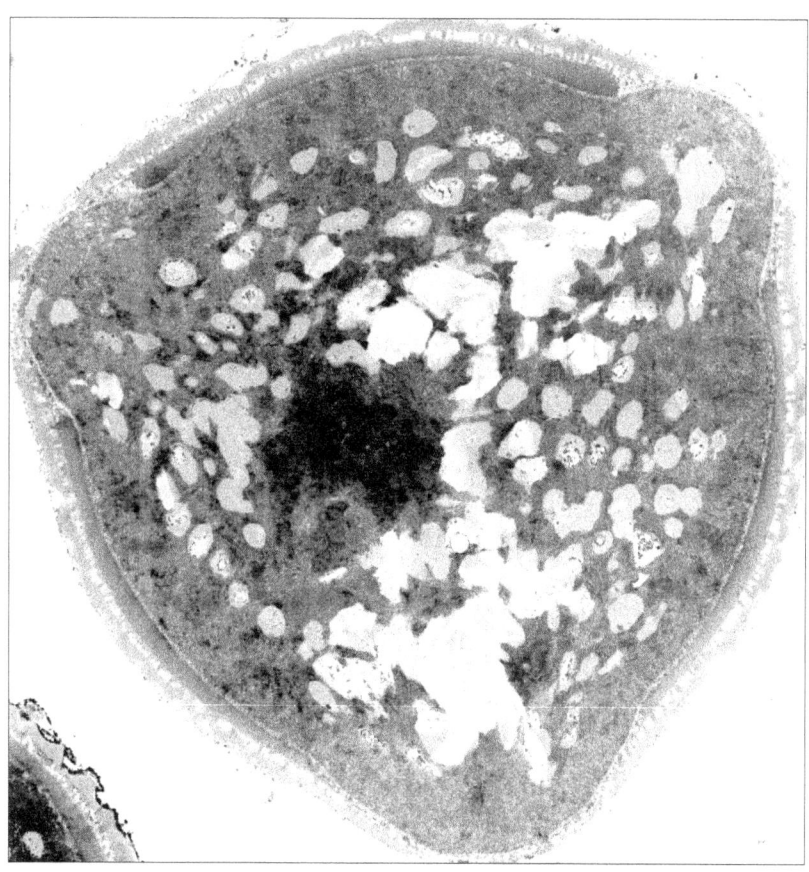

Figure 31. TEM section of *Meliotus officinalis* pollen from the B2 elbow. Lewis, 1997.

pollinated ones." In other words, the pollen in the B2 elbow was brought there by insects and not pulled in from the air.

Analysis identified five types of pollen, two of which made up 98.8% of the quantity found: *Grindelia squarrosa* (62.24%; Figure 29A) and *Meilotus officinalis* (36.56%; Figure 29B). Both are insect pollinated. Two others were found (*Verbesina encelioides*, family Asteraceae; *Sphaeralcea coccinea*, family Malavaceae) at very low percentages, bringing the total of insect pollen types to 99.9%. The time of pollination for these plants corresponds to the period during which the engine of the crashed plane was outdoors in the storage yard.

Pollen of only one wind-pollinated species, *Pinus edulis*, was found in the fuel unit. Its pollen is ubiquitous in the air wherever it grows. Further, an air sampler operating in Hobbs, New Mexico recorded abundant pollen of Poaceae (grasses) and *Juniperus* (juniper) in the air (Lewis et al, 1990) and yet none was found in the B2 elbow. From this evidence Lewis (1997, p. 388) concludes, "These observations reinforce the conclusion that the pollen part of the mass could not have accumulated either suddenly or over time from the air while the plane was in operation, and therefore the mass must be a post-crash accumulation."

The team subjected the material from the B2 elbow to further experiments to determine the effect of heat on pollen color (Graham, 1997a, b, c; figures 3-5). Pollen is known to darken when heated. As noted, the pollen grains from the tube were a glistening bright yellow. In the experiment, pre-heated pollen of *Hibiscus rosa-sinensis* (family Malvaceae) was the typical bright yellow color. After four hours at only 80° C, the grains became a dark-yellowish brown and their glistening coating and interconnecting strands disappeared. Consistent with other data, these results suggested that the pollen in the mass of organic material found in the B2 elbow was unrelated to the cause of the accident.

Trichomes. Another component of the organic mass in the B2 elbow was numerous stellate trichomes. These were studied in a manner comparable to the pollen, namely, identification using LM and SEM to compare the composition of the material in the tube with that of the flora growing in the storage yard, and heat experiments to determine the effect of high temperatures (Bates et al., 1997). The trichomes in the B2 elbow, like the pollen, proved to be *Sphaeralcea coccinea* present in the adjacent flora (Figures 23, 32, 33). FTIR demonstrated that the organic matrix enclosing the pollen, trichomes, leaf and other debris was from *Sphaeralcea* mixed with a honey-like nectar (Liddell, 1997). With regard to survival at "temperatures in excess of 593° C at the time of the crash, trichomes of *S. coccinea* were heated to temperature of 93°, 204°, and 315° C for periods of one-half hour. At the highest temperature studied, the trichomes became distorted, charred, and brittle, indicating that they could not have survived the temperatures if they had been present prior to the crash" (p. 385).

Soil. During the course of the trial, the plaintiffs suggested that a supplemental or alternative cause of the crash was the accumulation of soil in the engine's fuel component. After

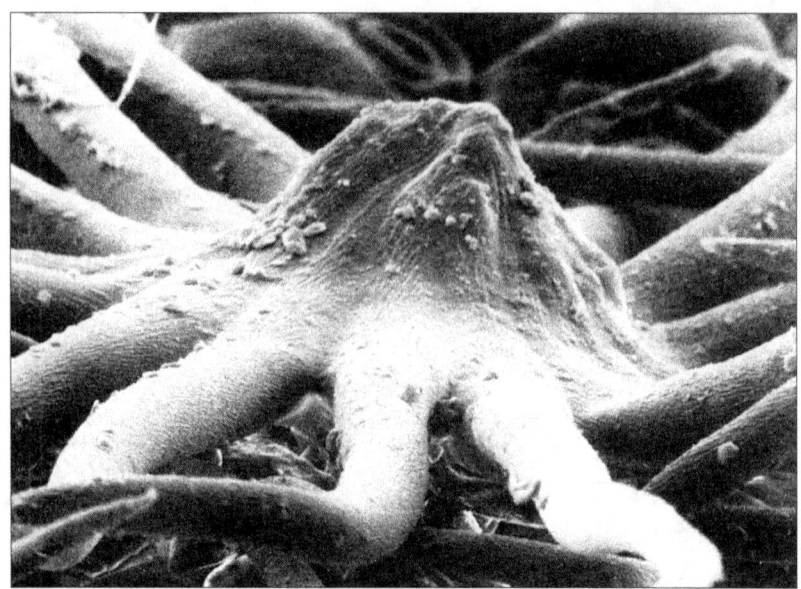

Figure 32. SEM of trichomes from *Sphaeralcea coccinea*. Bates et al., 1997.

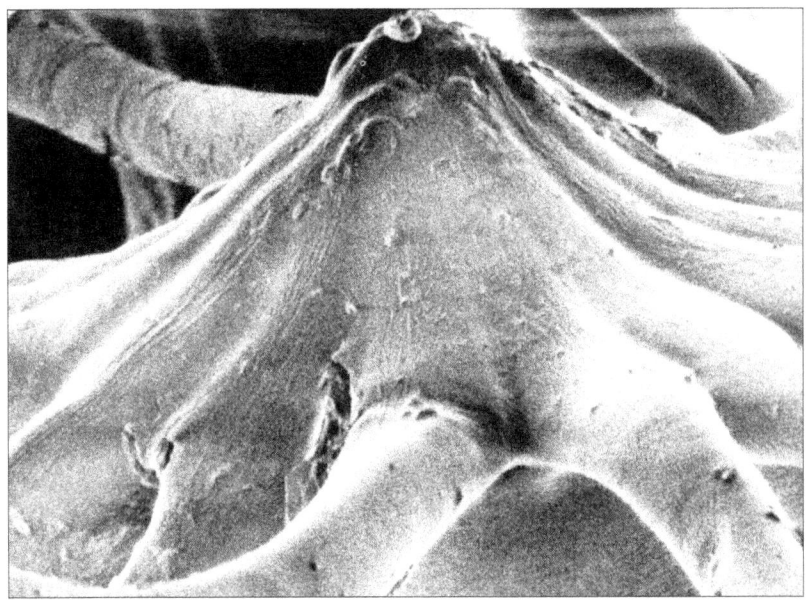

Figure 33. SEM of trichome from the B2 elbow. Bates et al., 1997.

the wreckage was put in the storage yard, soil was dumped over the parts to prevent leakage of fuel and possible fire. Analyses revealed that the composition of the dumped soil was of a general silicate type and similar to that in the storage yard. Further, had the soil been subjected to the heat of the engine—that is, present before the crash—the iron in the soil would have oxidized to a red color.

Soil samples were taken from the Ruidoso airport, the crash site in the adjacent mountains, and the dirt runway in Sand Springs, Montana. At Sand Springs, soil from both ends of the airstrip from which the plane landed and took off and the hanger where it parked was collected. The soil samples were heated to 1000° C and compared by a standard Redness Rating (RR). They all turned red at approximately 500° C, while the soil in the B2 elbow was not red (Daugherty, 1997). The plaintiffs and defendants each studied the soils by EDAX analysis and found them to be sandy. Daugherty (1997) observes that "nearly every soil in the world is made of silicate minerals" and "no evidence was found for the presence of soil in a pre-crash period that would have interfered with the operation of the airplane" (p. 401).

A plausible alternative. Based on the testing and analyses just described, the plant and other evidence seemed to prove overwhelmingly that the debris in the B2 elbow was a post-crash accumulation. However, "contrary to the presumption of innocence in criminal trials, in civil trials like this one, in which a plaintiff advances a theory, it frequently is not enough for a defendant just to counter the theory. Many times it is also necessary to give the jury a plausible alternative explanation for what they are seeing and what they are being told" (Brunk, 1997, p. 379).

As above, study of the biological mass in the B2 elbow established that the debris consisted of pollen and plant fragments from insect-pollinated plants, trichomes, nectar, and soil from the immediate vicinity of the storage yard. The explanation for the source seems obvious but, as Brunk (1997) noted, in a jury trial where other causes are vigorously being presented, it is desirable to make the alternative as convincing as possible. A significant step was taken in this direction when remains of the bee *Osmia gaudiosa* was found in parts of the fuel component (Figure 34), along with a hair from the head of *Ashmeadiella* that matched those from the elbow itself (Figure 35). With these, a compelling possibility came into focus: that the organic debris in the B2 elbow might be a post-crash bee's nest.

The behavior of bees provided further context. Over 21,000 kinds of bees have been identified and, in contrast to general perception, the majority of them are solitary. They work, build, and tend nests with pollen and nectar as single females unassisted by workers. Leaf-cutter bees (family Megachilidae, of which the genus *Ashmeadiella* is part) use pre-formed, tube-like tunnels in which to build their nests and often line those tunnels with plant fragments and resin. According to Rosen and Eickwort (1977, p. 396), "the presence of the branched hair in the pollen clump left no doubt that the blockage in the B2 elbow was indeed the remnants of a nest of *Ashmeadiella*." Such a nest would have been completely incinerated if present in the tube during operation of the plane at the time of the crash. With this information, all of the pieces of the puzzle fell into place: the nature of the organic matter, the means and agency by which it had arrived in the B2 elbow, and the reason it could not have been in the elbow prior to the accident.

Figure 34. *Osmia gaudiosa* bee from a cocoon in the B2 elbow. Bates et al.,1997.

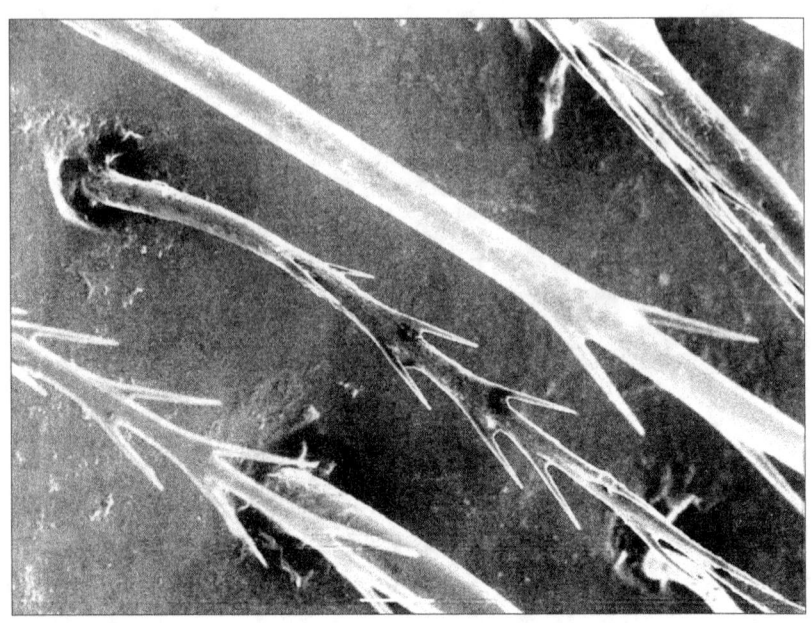

Figure 35. SEM of hair of the bee *Ashmeadiella* found in the pollen clump of the B2 elbow. Bates et al.,1997.

ENDNOTES

1   When two formations of the same age at different locations
are found to be at significantly different elevations it suggests
a fault probably runs through the intervening area. The
disruption can abut porous oil-bearing layers (e.g., shale)
against non-porous rocks (e.g., marble, granite) resulting
in a 'stratigraphic trap' and the formation of oil pools.

2   It may not be readily apparent but gymnosperms still compete
well today in dry habitats. The principal areas where they are
the main vegetation are in the boreal forest or taiga across
northern Europe, southern Canada, and the northern U.S.
and on high mountain slopes to the south as in eastern and
western North America. These regions experience four to six
months of winter when moisture is frozen as snow and ice, or is
unavailable in permafrost soils, or drains quickly from the coarse
soils and steep slopes before it can be absorbed. High northern
and alpine environments are not climatically arid but they are
physiologically dry and this is where modern gymnosperms benefit
from a competitive edge imparted by their ancient ancestors.

3   For those not familiar with seed dispersal in *Amorphophalus* and *Rafflesia*, those of the former are relatively large (larger than most carrion beetles) and are not sticky. In the latter, however,

"Frugivory and seed dispersal by vertebrates suggest they may be major dispersers of *Rafflesia keithii*, which has huge, indehiscent fruits with numerous tiny seeds in an oily pulp. The morphological characters of the fruits of Rafflesiaceae clearly indicate a zoochorouas dispersal. The many-seeded berries are sometimes brightly colored. The seeds have a fleshy, slimy or even sticky pulp; and seed dispersal has been reported by the tree-shrew (*Tupaia tana*) and squirrel (*Callosciurus notatus*). We encountered a fruit of *R. philippensis* in an advanced state of decay ... and after removing some of the decaying fruit wall we noticed numerous ants (*Technomyrmex* sp. and *Pheidologeton* sp.) These ants were carrying *Rafflesia* seeds away from the fruits which contain thousands of tiny seeds in the indehiscent berries" (Pelser et al., 2013; quotes from Yatskievych, personal communication, 7 September 2018).

4   https://en.wikipedia.org/wiki/Shanidar_cave based on the Smithsonian Shanidar pages- http://www/ mnh.si/anthro/humanorigins/ha/shanidar.html

REFERENCES

Algeo, T. J., R. A. Berner, J. P. Maynard, and S. E. Scheckler. 1995. Late Devonian oceanic anoxic events and biotic crises: "rooted" in the evolution of vascular land plants. GSA Today 5: 45, 64-66.

Algeo, T. J. and S. E. Scheckler. 1998. Terrestrial-marine teleconnections in the Devonian: links between the evolution of land plants, weathering processes, and marine anoxic events. Philosophical Transactions of the Royal Society (London), B 353: 113-130.

Algeo, T. J., S. E. Schleckler, and J. B. Maynard. 2000. Effects of the Middle to Late Devonian spread of vascular land plants on weathering regimes, marine biota, and glacial climate. In: P. G. Gensel and D. Edwards (eds.), Plants invade the land: evolutionary and environmental approaches. Columbia University Press, New York. p. 213-236.

Allwood, A. C., M. T. Rosing, D. T. Flannery, J. A. Hurowitz, and C. M. Heirwegh. 2018. Reassessing evidence of life in 3,700-million-year-old rocks of Greenland. Nature, https://doi.org/10.1038/d41586-018-0610-4.

Aubert, M. et al. (+ 9 authors). 2014. Pleistocene cave art from Solawesi, Indonesia. Nature 514: 223-227.

Baden, M.M. 1983. Plenary session: the Lindbergh kidnapping revisited: Forensic sciences then and now. Journal of Forensic Sciences 8: 1035-1037.

Bates, D. M., G. J. Anderson, and R. D. Lee. 1997. Forensic botany: trichome evidence. In: A. Graham (ed.), Symposium on forensic chemistry, soil analysis, entomology, botany, palynology, and other aspects of non-genetic-marker biology. Journal of Forensic Sciences 42: 380-386.

Bock, J. H. and D. O. Norris. 1997. Forensic botany: an under-utilized resource. In: A. Graham (ed.), Symposium on forensic chemistry, soil analysis, entomology, botany, palynology, and other aspects of non-genetic-marker biology. Journal of Forensic Sciences 42: 364-367.

Bock, J. H. and D. O. Norris. 2016. Forensic plant science. Academic Press. Elsevier, Amsterdam.

Breeze, R. G., B. Budowle, and S. E. Schutzer (eds.). 2005. Microbial forensics. Elsevier, Amsterdam.

Brunk, S. K. 1997. The Ruidoso plane crash—the background and the trial verdict. In: A. Graham (ed.), Symposium on forensic chemistry, soil analysis, entomology, botany, palynology, and other aspects of non-genetic-marker biology. Journal of Forensic Sciences 42: 378-379.

Coyle, H. M. (ed.). 2005. Forensic botany, principles and applications of criminal casework. CRC Press, Boca Raton.

Crubézy, E. and K. Trinkaus. 1992. Shanidar 1: a case of hyperostoic disease (DISH) in the middle Paleolithic. American Journal of Physical Anthropology 89: 411-420.

Daugherty, L. A. 1997. Soil science contribution to an airplane crash investigation, Ruidoso, New Mexico. Journal of Forensic Sciences 42: 401-405.

Douglas, I. 2015. Neanderthal 'flower children' burials theory debunked. https://www.telegraph.co.uk/news/earth/environment/archaeology/11919272/Neanderthal-flower-children-burials-theory-debunked.html

Evans, C. 1996. The casebook of forensic detection. John Wiley, New York.

Finlayson, C. 2019. The smart Neanderthal: bird catching, cave art, and the cognitive revolution. Oxford University Press, Oxford.

Graham, A. 1962. The role of fungal spores in palynology. Journal of Paleontology 36: 60-68.

Graham, A. 1976. Studies in Neotropical paleobotany. II. The Miocene communities of Veracruz, Mexico. Annals of the Missouri Botanical Garden 63: 787-842.

Graham, A. (ed.). 1997a. Symposium on forensic chemistry, soil analysis, entomology, botany, palynology, and other aspects of non-genetic-marker biology. Journal of Forensic Sciences 42: 363-405.

Graham, A. 1997b Introduction to the symposium papers. Journal of Forensic Sciences 42: 363.

Graham, A. 1997c. Forensic palynology and the Ruidoso, New Mexico plane crash—the pollen evidence II. Journal of Forensic Sciences 42: 391-393.

Graham, A. 2010. Benjamin Carroll Tharp (1885-1964), remembering a life fashioned of events and circumstances. Lundellia 13: 3-9.

Graham, A. 2011. A natural history of the New World, the ecology and evolution of plants in the Americas. University of Chicago Press, Chicago.

Graham, A. in prep. Migrations, 100 million years, 100,000 miles. University of Chicago Press, Chicago.

Graham, A., S. A. Graham, and D. Geer. 1968. Palynology and systematics of Cuphea (Lythraceae). I. Morphology and ultrastructure of the pollen wall. American Journal of Botany 55: 1080-1088.

Graham, A., J. Nowicke, J. J. Skvarla, S. A. Graham, V. Patel, and S. Lee. 1985. Palynology and systematics of the Lythraceae. I. Introduction and genera Adenaria through Ginoria. American Journal of Botany 72: 1012-1031.

Graham, S. 1997. Anatomy of the Lindbergh kidnapping. In: A. Graham (ed.), Symposium on forensic chemistry, soil analysis, entomology, botany, palynology, and other aspects of non-genetic-marker biology. Journal of Forensic Sciences 42: 368-377.

Graham, S. 2006. Crime-solving plants. Plant Science Bulletin 52: 78-84.

Graham, S. and A. Graham. 2014. Ovary, fruit, and seed morphology of the Lythraceae. International Journal of Plant Sciences 175: 202-240.

Hall, D. W. and J. H. Byrd (eds.). 2012. Forensic botany, a practical guide. Wiley-Blackwell, West Sussex.

Hallam, A. and P. B. Wignall. 1997. Mass extinctions and their aftermath. Oxford University Press, Oxford.

Harari, Y. N. 2015. Sapiens, a brief history of humankind. HarperCollins, New York.

Hawksworth, D. L. and P. E. J. Wiltshire. 2011. Forensic mycology: the use of fungi in criminal investigations. Forensic Science International 206: 1-11.

Henshilwood, C. S., F. d'Errico, K. L. van Niekerk, L. Dayet, A. Queffelec, and L. Pollarolo. 2018. An abstract drawing from the 73,000-year-old levels at Blombos Cave, South Africa. Nature, https://www.nature.com/articles/s41586-018-0514-3

Hoffmann, D. L. et al. (+ 13 authors). 2018. U-Th dating of carbonate crusts reveals Neanderthal origin of Iberian cave art. Science 359: 912-915.

Iversen, J. 1949. The influence of prehistoric man on vegetation. Danmarks Geologiske Underøgelse 3: 1-25.

Iversen, J. 1956. Forest clearance in the Stone Age. Scientific American 194: 36-41.

Kesling, R. V. and A. Graham. 1962. *Ischadites* is a dasycladacean alga. Journal of Paleontology 36: 943-952.

Leroi-Gourham, A. 1975. The flowers found with Shanidar IV: a Neanderthal burial in Iraq. Science 190: 562-564.

Levy, T. (ed.). 2001. The archaeology of society in the Holy Land. Leicester University Press, London.

Lewis, W. H. 1997. Pollen composition in a crashed plane's engine. Journal of Forensic Sciences 42: 387-390.

Lewis, W. H., A. B. Dixit, and W. A. Ward. 1990. Distribution and incident of North American pollen aeroallergens. American Journal of Otolaryngology 12: 205-226.

Liddell, C. M. 1997. Field sampling and chemical analysis. Journal of Forensic Sciences 42: 398-400.

McGhee, G. R., Jr. 1996. The Late Devonian Mass Extinction. Columbia University Press, New York.

Nadel, D. et al. (+ 11 authors). 2013. Earliest floral grave lining from 13,700—11,700-y-old Natufian burials at Raqefet Cave, Mt. Carmel, Israel. Proceedings of the National Academy of Sciences USA 110: 11774-11778.

The National Geographic. 2016. The real CSI. The National Geographic, July 2016.

Nature Editorials. 2018. Prior art, the earliest known drawing—crayon on a rock shard—suggests early humans engaged in abstract art. Nature 561: 149.

Nutman, A. P., V. C. Bennett, C. R. L. Friend, M. J. Van Kranendock, and A. R. Chivas. 2016. Rapid emergence of life shown by discovery of 3,700-million-year-old microbial structures. Nature 537: 535-538.

Pelser, P. H., D. L. Nickrent, J. R. C. Callado, and J. F. Barcelona. 2013. Mt Banahaw reveals: the resurrection and neotypification of the name *Rafflesia lagascae* (Rafflesiaceae) and clues to the dispersal of *Rafflesia* seeds. Phytotaxa 131: 35-40.

Pettitt, J. and C. B. Beck. 1968. *Archaeosperma arnoldii*—a cupulate seed from the Upper Devonian of North America. Contributions from the Museum of Paleontology, University of Michigan 22: 139-154.

Pettitt, P. B. 2002. The Neanderthal dead: exploring mortuary variability in Middle Palaeolithic Eurasia. Before Farming 2002/1 (4): 1-19.

Piperno, D. R. 2006. Quaternary environmental history and agricultural impact on vegetation in Central America. In: A. Graham (ed.), Latin American biogeography—causes and effects. Annals of the Missouri Botanical Garden 93: 274-296.

Piperno, D. R. and D. M. Pearsall. 1998. The origins of agriculture in the lowland Neotropics. Academic Press, New York.

Rosen, J. G. and G. C. Eickwort. 1997. The entomological evidence. Journal of Forensic Sciences 42: 394-397.

Rothwell, G. W., S. E. Scheckler, and G. H. Gillepsie. 1989. *Elkinsia* gen. nov., a Late Devonian gymnosperm with cupulate ovules. Botanical Gazette 150: 170-189.

Schultes, R. E., W. M. Klein, T. Plowman, and T. E. Lockwood. 1974. *Cannabis*: an example of taxonomic neglect. Botanical Museum Leaflets, Harvard University, 23: 337-367.

Scott, R. A. and E. A. Wheeler. 1982. Fossil woods from the Eocene Clarno Formation of Oregon. International Association of Wood Anatomists Bulletin 3: 135-154.

Smithsonian Insider. 2009. Research collection of pollen grains given to Smithsonian Tropical Research Institute. Smithsonian Insider, 6 June 2009.

Solecki, R. S. 1971. Shanidar, the first flower people. Knopf, New York.

Solecki, R. S. 1975. Shanidar IV, a Neanderthal flower burial in northern Iraq. Science 190: 880-881.

Sommer, D. J. 1999. The Shanidar IV 'flower burial': a re-evaluation of Neanderthal burial ritual. Cambridge Archaeological Journal 9: 127-129.

Stewart, T. D. 1959. The restored Shanidar I skull. Smithsonian Institution Annual Report for 1958: 473-480.

Streel, M., M. V. Caputo, S. Lovboziak, and J. H. G. Melo. 2000. Late Frasnian-Famennian climate: based on palynomorph analyses and the question of the Late Devonian glaciation. Earth-Science Reviews: 52: 121-173.

Stromberg, J. 2013. Archaeologists find evidence of flowers buried in a 12,000-year-old cemetery. https://www.Smithsonianmag.com/science-nature/archaeologists-find-evidence-4280031

Tanay, E. 1983. The Lindbergh kidnapping- a psychiatric view. Journal of Forensic Sciences 8: 1044-1048.

Taylor, T. N., E. L. Taylor, and M. Krings. 2009. Paleobotany, the biology and evolution of fossil plants. 2nd ed. Academic Press, New York.

Trinkaus, E. 1983. The Shanidar Neanderthals. Academic Press, New York.

Van Zuilen, M. A. 2018. Proposed early signs of life not set in stone. Nature, https://doi.org/10.1038/d41586-018-06994-x

Wood, B. 2019. How Neanderthal minds took flight. Nature 566: 35-36.

ADDITIONAL READINGS

Australian Museum. 2009. Decomposition—forensic evidence. Updated 12 November 2009. http://australianmuseum. net.au/decomposition-forensic-evidence

Bock, J. H., M. A. Lane, and D. O. Norris. 1988. Plant food cells in gastric contents for use in forensic investigations: a laboratory manual. U.S. Department of Justice, National Institute of Justice Research Report, January 1988.

Bouman, F. and W. Meijer. 1994. Comparative structure of ovules and seeds in Rafflesiaceae. Plant Systematics and Evolution 193: 187-212.

Bryant, V. M., Jr. and G. D. Jones. 2006. Forensic palynology: current status of a rarely used technique in the United States of America. Forensic Science International 163: 183-197.

Bryant, V. M., Jr., and D. C. Mindenhall. 1990. Forensic palynology in the United States of America. Palynology 14: 193-208.

Committee on identifying the needs of the forensic science community in the United States: a path forward. 2009. Final Report, Federally Funded NCJRS Proposal 2006-DN-BX-0001.

The Economist. 2013. Silica extracted from rice husks makes for greener tyres. The Economist, 5 January 2013. p. 65.

The Economist. 2018. Criminal Justice, Against pessimism, there is nothing inevitable about America's over-use of prisons. The Economist, 20 October 2018, pp. 12-13.

Forensic Botany. Web site created in 2002 by J. V. Dommlen as a project in the WEB Literacy for the Natural Sciences class, Dalhousie University, Halifax, Canada; last updated April 2002.

Forensic Magazine. 2012. 'Southwest pollen' linked to 1979 NY cold case. Forensic Magazine, 01 May 2012 (source: Russell Contreras, The Associated Press).

Gaillard, Y. and G. Pepin. 1999. Poisoning by plant material: review of human cases and analytical determination of main toxins by high-performance liquid chromatography-(tandem) mass spectrometry. Journal of Chromatography B, Biomedical Sciences Applications 733: 181-229.

Greenwood, V. 2016. Beyond reasonable doubt. National Geographic, July 2016, p. 30-56.

The Guardian. 2004. Jail for torso case people smuggler. 27 July 2004 (United Kingdom).

Keefe, P.R. 2013. Snoop dreams: how private investigation became an industry. The New Yorker, 5 October 2013, p. 61-66.

Lipscomb, B. L. and G. M. Diggs, Jr. 1998. The use of animal-dispersed seeds and fruits in forensic botany. SIDA 18: 335-346.

Mildenhall, D. 1998. It takes just a few specks of dust and you are caught. Canadian Association of Palynologists Newsletter 21: 18-21.

Milne, L. 2005. A grain of truth. How pollen brought a murderer to justice. Reed New Holland Publications, Sydney.

PBS Newshour. 2013. From Guatemalan soil, scientists unearth signs of genocide. Air date 8 May 2013.

Ponman, B. E. and R. W. Bussmann (eds.). 2011. Medicinal plants and the legacy of Richard E. Schultes. Missouri Botanical Garden, St. Louis.

Pope, F. 1935. State of New Jersey vs. Bruno Richard Hauptmann. Trial transcript, 1935: 3796.

Potgieter, L. J., M. Gaertner, P. J. O'Farrell, and D. M. Rcihardson. 2019. Does vegetation structure influence criminal activity? Insights from Cape Town, South Africa. https://escholarship.org/uc/item/9j9290x8

Rhode, D. L. 2015. The trouble with lawyers. Oxford University Press, Oxford.

Ross, A. and D. Robins. 1989. The life and death of a druid prince. Summit Books, New York.

Sofiyanti, N. and C. C. Yen. 2012. Morphology of ovule, seed and pollen grain of *Rafflesia* R. Br. (Rafflesiaceae). Bangladesh Journal of Plant Taxonomy 19: 109-117.

Szibor, R., C. Schubert, R. Schöning, D. Krause, and U. Wendt. 1998. Pollen analysis reveals murder season. Nature 395: 449-450.

Trenchard, T. W. State of New Jersey vs. Bruno Richard Hauptmann. Trial transcript, 1935: 3805.

Ward, J., R. Peakall, S. R. Gilmore, and J. Robertson 2005. A molecular identification system for grasses: a novel technology for forensic botany. Forensic Science International 152: 121-131.

Weintraub, A. 2008. Nanotech: pollinating the crime scene. Businessweek, 18 August 2008.

Yoon, C. K. 1993. Botanical witness for the prosecution. Science 260: 894-895.

INFORMATION ON OTHER METHODOLOGIES

BLOODSTAIN PATTERNS

Gupta, S. 2017. Criminology: written in blood, bloodstain pattern analysis is used by forensic scientists to help reconstruct violent crimes. Efforts are underway to root the often subjective practice in science. Nature 549: S24-S25.

DISEASE INJECTION/ PHYLOGENETIC FORENSICS

Bhattacharya, S. 2014. Science in court: disease detectives. Nature 506: 424-426.

DNA

Abbott, A. 2013. Bringing out the dead...how a DNA forensics team cracked a grisly puzzle. Nature 503: 465.

Callaway, E. 2018. Privacy concerns over DNA used for crime investigation. Nature 562: 315-316.

Nature Editorial. 2018. The ethics of catching criminals using their family's DNA/ Family connections. Nature 557: 5.

Nature Editorials. 2018. Proceed with caution, proposed molecular testing of a person's age highlights difficult questions for scientists and society. Nature 561: 5.

HANDWRITING, TYPEWRITING, SHOEPRINTS/FOOTWEAR AND TIRE TRACK EXAMINATION

Forensic Science Communications. 2001. Handwriting, typewriting, shoeprints, and tire treads. Forensic Science Communications 3(2), https://archives. fbi.gov/archives/about-us/lab/forensic-science-communications/fsc/april2001/held.htm

Fuller, J. 2014. How impression evidence works. http:// science.howstuffworks.com/impression-evidence.htm

Garrett, A. 2013. Tire tread and tire track evidence. Video, https://youtu.be/dhkSlJadfPs

Wikipedia. 2013. A simplified guide to footware & tire track examination. http://en.wikipedia.org/w/index. php?title=forensic_tire_tread_evidence&oldid=536311123

FORENSIC PSYCHOLOGY

Bartol, C. R. and A. M. Bartol. 2014. Introduction to forensic psychology: research and application. SAGE Publications, Thousand Oaks (CA).

SCANNERS

The Economist. 2012. Reviving autopsy, Medical
technology: Using a scanner, rather than a scalpel,
has the potential to make autopsies faster, cheaper
and more accurate. The Economist, 3 March 2012.

TIME OF DEATH ESTIMATES
VIA ENZYME ANALYSIS

Harkup, K. 2018. Making the monster, the science behind
Mary Shelley's Frankenstein. Bloomsbury, London. p. 145.

PRIVACY

Artz, K. 2013. Congress approves domestic use of aerial
surveillance drones. http://news/heartland.org/
print/123986

CNNMoney. 2014. The 6 companies behind the drone
revolution. 16 August 2014. https://money.cnn.com/
gallery/investing/2014/08/06/drone-stocks/index.html

CNNMoney. 2014. Camera on cops: coming to a town near
you. 14 March 2014. https://money.cnn.com/2014/03/14/
technology/security/cameras-on-cops/index.html

The Economist. 2014. The west wind blows afresh,
a cheap alternative to satellites is starting to
take off. The Economist, 30 August 2014.

The Economist. 2014. Computer spying, attack of
the cybermen, sophisticated viruses will be the
workhorses of 21st-century spying. But there should
be rules. The Economist, 29 November 2014.

Fink, E. 2013. Hackers control car's steering and brakes. CNNMoney, https://money.cnn.com/2014/08/01/technology/security/most-hackable-cars/index.html

Khatchadourian, R. 2015. We know how you feel, computers are learning to read emotion, and the business world can't wait. The New Yorker, 19 January 2015.

Lake, H. 2014. Portland company apologizes to Seattle woman for flying drone in front of her apartment window. https://katu.com/news/local/portland-company-apologizes-to-seattle-woman-for-flying-drone-in-front-of-her-apartment-window

Lejacq, Y. 2013. Game on for surveillance? Privacy advocates concerned over new consoles. https://www.nbcnews.com/technolog/game-surveillance-privacy-advocates-concerned-over-new-consoles-6C10732136

Moore, D. 2013. Focusing on crime, success of surveillance in Boston is cited in support for linking cameras here. https://www.stltoday.com/news/local/metro/success-of-boston-surveillance-photos-cited-in-support-for-broader-system-in-st-louis/article_437c5108-7f99-5d7e-94ff-979c38cf645e.html

United States Institute of Peace. 2005. Terrorism and counter-terrorism web links. http://www/usip.org/publications/terrorism-and-counter-terrorism-web-links

ABUSES AND CONCERNS

Costandi, M. 2013. Evidence-based justice: corrupted memory. Nature 500: 268-270.

Mejia, R. 2017. Label the limits of forensic science. Nature 544: 17.

Nature. 2017. Forensic-data check, in Seven Days, 29 November 2017, https://www/nature.com/articles/d41586-017-07513-0

Nature Editorials. 2011. Courtroom drama, forensic science faces rough justice on both sides of the Atlantic. Nature 471: 548.

Nature Editorials. 2018. False testimony. Nature 557: 612.

Reardon, S. 2014. Faulty forensic science under fire. Nature 506: 13-14.

Wikipedia. 2014. Innocence Project. http://en.wikipedia.org/wiki/Innocence_Project

ILLUSTRATION CREDITS

Photographs unless otherwise credited are by Shirley A. Graham. The illustration of Asteroid 243 Ida and its moon for Mass Extinctions was photographed from NASA's Galileo Space Craft on August 28, 1983 from a distance of 6755 miles (see also A. Graham, 1999, *Late Cretaceous and Cenozoic History of North American Vegetation*, Figure 2.23, Oxford University Press, Oxford; photograph courtesy The Jet Propulsion Laboratory, Pasadena, California).

The photograph by Marcos Guerra that comprises Figure 19 appears on https://insider.si.edu/2009/07/research-collection-of-pollen-grains-given-to-smithsonian-tropical-research-institute/

Figure 26 was obtained from Wikipedia and can be found at: https://en.wikipedia.org/wiki/Spindletop#/media/file:Lucas_gusher.jpg

FROM NONFICTION TO FICTION

FROM NONFICTION TO FICTION

As this book suggests, plant evidence has been used to detect physical and climatological changes and evolutionary patterns in the geological record. It has played a role in clarifying the behavioral nature and legacy of *Homo sapiens'* earliest human associates, competitors, and mating partners. Plant anatomy was fundamental in solving "the crime of the century." Finally, pollen and spores (palynology), seeds, trichomes, soils, and fibers helped assess the cause of a fatal airplane accident with significant implications for this type of litigation.

Diverse as they are, these real-life mysteries and their plant-related solutions don't capture the full applicability of plant science as it is applies to investigations of life and death. For this it is convenient, informative, novel, and perhaps even entertaining to recount actual methodologies using three fictional situations that put forensic plant science on full display. These situations are recounted in the dastardly deeds of three mysteries (a fourth in the series is currently underway). I hope you will enjoy *Gateway to Murder, Season of Discontent,* and *Mass Extinctions,* summaries of which follow.

GATEWAY
TO
MURDER

A
Green Mystique
Forensic Mystery

ALAN GRAHAM

Gateway to Murder

When Armillas Longoria is found stabbed to death on the walkway of the St. Louis Arch, John Ramming's team of brilliant misfits at the Division of Criminal Investigation Services is immediately called in. The murder weapon is missing, but the autopsy makes clear it's no ordinary knife; in fact, the team begins to suspect that it might be an rare artifact of incalculable historical significance. In the course of their expert analysis, they discover that the mud clumped on the victim's sleeve is also unusual, containing a mix of spores, pollen, seeds and other debris so distinctive that it alone might pinpoint the killer. Concerned by the complexity of the evidence and the prime suspect's convincing alibi, prosecutors refuse to bring the case to trial. Though it takes time, justice ultimately prevails in the 100th case on the astute if cantankerous Ramming's watch.

SEASON
OF
DISCONTENT

A
Green Mystique
Forensic Mystery

ALAN GRAHAM

Season of Discontent

John Ramming's elite and idiosyncratic team at the St. Louis Division of Criminal Investigation Services is stretched to the limit when three major crimes occur within 24 hours. The corpse of university professor Charles Bradshaw is found with a crudely fashioned crown of thorns and thirty silver dollars on its chest, suggesting a religious motive. Though the sudden disappearance of Assistant Attorney General Brad Zimmerman is a relief to those he abused, his high-profile position and access to sensitive information demands that he be found. College student Melissa Krauss was last seen getting into the car of an eccentric man that school security has been allowing to sleep in his car in the campus parking lot; since she, like Zimmerman, may still be alive, every moment is critical. Plant materials become key forensic clues as DCIS races against time to analyze and act on the evidence.

MASS
EXTINCTIONS

A
Green Mystique
Forensic Mystery

ALAN GRAHAM

Mass Extinctions

With John Ramming's partial retirement, Ito Sebacious becomes Commander of the St. Louis Division of Criminal Investigation Services as the DCIS faces its most complex crime to date. It begins when the four bodies are found dead in a freezer in an abandoned city warehouse. Using their network of contacts and databases, the team discovers other killings that share the same apparent motive: though the cases are spread across the country, all of the victims are known to be individuals that have despoiled sites or landscapes as well as people's lives. The murders—effected by freezing, scorching heat, and lava extrusion among other means—parallel the causes of prehistoric mass extinctions brought into popular consciousness through the lectures of Nobel laureate Paul Matson, who is concerned that a sixth extinction event is underway. Are these connections mere coincidence, or do they signal the work of an underground crusade?

ACKNOWLEDGMENTS

Information on *Amorphophalus* and *Rafflesia* was provided by Fred Barrie, Charles Davis, Marceia Mora, Mary Morello, and George Yatskievych. In addition to providing many of the photographs, Shirley A. Graham also read the manuscript and generously offered many helpful suggestions.

This project began as a nonfiction manuscript on investigative and forensic plant science and ended as a four-volume series comprising this volume and three fictional mysteries. It was a learning experience best attempted with the guidance of an experienced and competent advisor. This guidance was graciously, patiently, gently and convincingly provided by Suzanne Fox of Bookstrategy Inc. (www.bookstrategy.com), an author in her own right as well as an experienced consulting editor for others. I am one of the many benefactors of her expertise and persistence, and as a "mature" student am very grateful for the fascinating education she has provided.

I am also grateful to cj Madigan of Shoebox Stories, whose design of this book so scrupulously brought its vision onto the printed page.

ABOUT THE AUTHOR

The author of over 150 papers and books, botanist ALAN GRAHAM received his training in botany and geology at the University of Texas and the University of Michigan before doing his postdoctoral work at Harvard and the University of Amsterdam. In addition to his research work, Dr. Graham spent more than four decades as a teacher, primarily at Kent State University. Since 2002, he has served as Curator of Paleobotany & Palynology at the Missouri Botanical Garden's Center for Conservation and Sustainable Development. Dr. Graham's honors include the Smithsonian Institution Jose Cuatrecasas Medal for Excellence in Tropical Botany and the British Museum of Natural History (London)/Marsh Trust award for Best Book in the Earth Sciences for 2018's *Land Bridges*. Dr. Graham is also the author of the mystery novels *Gateway to Murder, Season of Discontent*, and *Mass Extinctions*, to which this book serves as a companion. Dr. Graham and his wife Shirley, also a scientist, live in St. Louis. For more information about the author and his work, please visit www.alangrahambooks.com.